BARK UP AND SMELL THE COFFEE

PAWS FUR PLAY MYSTERIES BOOK TWO

STELLA ST CLAIRE

PAWS FUR PLAY MYSTERIES

Home is Where the Bark Is

Bark Up and Smell the Coffee

The Bark of the Town

A PAWS FUR PLAY MYSTERY

Bark
Up And Smell
The
Coffee

Stella St. Claire

CONTENTS

BLURB

Willow Wells is officially an entrepreneur. With the first phase of her dog gym's renovation complete, and a success, Willow is ready for more. A doggie spa to be exact. The plan is to win an upcoming dog show, not only giving her the funds for the expansion but a national advertising campaign with the winning dog, Lady Valkyrie. Everything is going according to plan—and Willow can see the future in all its gold medal and dog grooming glory—until Terry Gib, Lady Valkyrie's owner, is accused of murder.

Willow thought that Terry had come to Pineview just for training, but it turns out Terry has ties to the town; a painful past that links her to a local bed and breakfast owner. And now that owner is dead. As Willow races to clear Terry and save their chance at victory with Lady Valkyrie, the rest of her life begins to fall apart too. Wednesday is distracted, her father is anxious, and Griffin, the man she's coming to depend on, is threatening to leave her—so he can woo her.

Now Willow is forced to make some big decisions: about who she trusts, who she should believe, and who she should date, before she loses it all forever.

THANK YOU!

Thank you for purchasing
"Bark Up And Smell The Coffee"
(Paws Fur Play Mysteries Book 2)

Sign-up to Stella's mailing list at:
www.StellaStClaire.com/newsletter

Discover more about Stella on:

Stella's Website: www.stellastclaire.com

Stella's Facebook: fb.com/stellastclaire

Stella's Goodreads: www.goodreads.com/Stella_StClaire

PROLOGUE

K aitlin Janes stared at the ceiling, willing herself to get out of bed. This was more than fatigue. It might be time to admit that she was getting sick. Maybe it was the flu? Was this the right season for it? She had several of the symptoms. She was exhausted, she had been feeling dizzy, and there was a ringing in her ears.

No. That was her alarm clock that was still ringing. She had been too tired to reach over the turn the buzzing off. She took a deep breath and moved her arm to hit the proper button. She hated feeling so sluggish and was dreading getting out from under her covers.

She promised herself a cup of nice warm coffee if she could force herself to get up. Though her body agreed reluctantly, she made her way to the kitchen. She looked around for a clean mug to pour the beverage she so desperately needed. Many of her mugs had been left around her apartment with the dregs of her past drinks still inside. So sue her, it wasn't the cleanest home in the world. She was a busy woman. She had a business to run and dogs to care for. She wasn't going to waste her time cleaning the part of her bed-and-breakfast that the guests didn't see. Besides, when even getting out of bed was a challenge, why would she waste the energy washing dishes?

She couldn't find a clean mug but opted to re-use a dirty one that had been hiding behind a pile of newspapers, a few cans of dog food, and a collection of corkscrews. She only ever used the mugs for coffee anyway, so it wasn't like it was really dirty, right?

She happily took a big swig of the drink, trying to wake herself up. It was funny that she felt so tired. She thought that she would have felt incredible today. She'd finally faced her past, and she should have felt a weight lifted from her shoulders. But, instead, her whole body felt heavy.

All right, she told herself, if you still feel this tired in the afternoon, you should call a doctor.

She had a few things she needed to do before she could afford to take a sick day though. Her morning routine always began with enjoying her coffee on the porch and walking her dog. Today would be no exception.

When they came back inside, she would make sure that the "breakfast" part of her bed-and-breakfast promise was fulfilled for both her human and canine visitors. But first, she would find the dog's leash. She had purposely chosen a fluorescent purple leash, so she would be able to find it if it got lost in the stacks of stuff in her apartment. Where was it hiding today? And why was this search so tiring?

She tried to think about the night before to see if she could dredge up the happy thoughts for strength but ended up bumping into a table and knocking over a pile of magazines and some jelly jars.

"Great," she muttered. "Another bruise."

She pushed the magazines to the side with her foot and was rewarded with finding the dog's leash. Then, she changed her clothes and topped her coffee off again before heading out of her apartment and towards the guest portion of the house.

Ordinarily, she would tidy the one or two items that were out of place in this section of the house. She liked for this to appear pristine and picture perfect, but she just didn't have the energy to care today.

"Polly," she called as she reached the front door.

She was glad the small Pekingese was used to the morning routine now and met her there. She didn't want to have to chase anything that morning.

They walked onto the front porch together, the fluffy dog staying near her feet. Usually, she would sit down and sip her coffee, waving at passersbys while her dog took care of business behind the rose bushes. Then, they would walk together.

However, today she remained standing. She wasn't confident that she would be willing to rise to her feet again if she sat down. She did wave to a few of the people who passed her.

She smiled as she always did when she thought about the prime location of her establishment. It was on Main Street and always had good foot traffic. This early in the morning, there were joggers and dog walkers who used the scenic road as their route. Many of them were like clockwork, always there at the same time.

Polly returned to Kaitlin, and she set her coffee down on the porch. At least this portion of the morning was the same as usual. She grabbed Polly's leash and clipped it onto her collar.

They began walking down the street, but as they reached the end of the block, Kaitlin wavered. She had a terrible cramping feeling inside her. It was a pain she had never experienced before.

Polly began whining. Kaitlin felt eyes upon her, but she couldn't be worried about them. Her knees were starting to give out, and she fell over.

A jogger with a birthmark on his face caught her. She wanted to thank him, but the words wouldn't come out.

"Is that Kaitlin?" a female voice asked. It sounded familiar. She knew that voice, but she was having trouble keeping track of her thoughts.

She could hear other voices asking what was wrong with her. Kaitlin was dimly aware that the answer was something very, very bad.

1

Willow Wells raised the coffee mug emblazoned with "Man's Best Friend's Bestie" to her mouth and took a sip of the steaming beverage that always brought her such joy in the morning. There was a light breezing blowing, and the chair on her porch was covered with comfy cushions.

"This is the life, isn't it?" she asked her dog.

Telescope yipped in agreement and jumped onto her lap. Her chihuahua-mix only had three legs, but he still made these leaps look easy. She rubbed his ears and savored her hot drink, smiling and enjoying the peace. She knew it might not last long because she had a big decision to make, but that could wait until after she finished her coffee.

She decided to sit back, which was easy in this soft chair, and enjoy the view. She could see the tall trees in the distant forest that gave Pineview its name. Closer by was a sight she enjoyed even more.

Her backyard housed her business, Paws Fur Play. It was a doggie gym where dogs could run and socialize, learn basic obedience, or train for competitions. It was also an area where Telescope could show off his moves on the obstacle course.

For a while, it seemed as if the business would never open – thanks to the complication of finding a dead body buried in her backyard. However, after clearing her contractor and friend's name and finding the real killer, construction was able to commence, and after just a few busy months, the gym was finished.

Willow shook her head. She didn't want to think about murders anymore. That was the past. She needed to focus on the future.

She looked through the large windows into the enclosed area of her training facility and watched the pups enjoying their free play time. Tails were wagging, and they looked content.

She wanted to keep an eye on the new trainers that she'd hired to assist her with dogs but was trying not to hover. She was confident that she had chosen good people to work with her. However, she had never needed to hire employees before and couldn't help being a bit nervous about it. She kept reminding herself that they were qualified trainers and that they had all been approved by Telescope. And besides, after facing a murderer, making sure employees followed her instructions should be easy.

She drained the last of the coffee in her cup and let out a little sigh.

"Well, I had the trainers come in so that I could do boss stuff," she said. "I guess I should get down to it, huh?"

Telescope barked in agreement. It was crazy how much of conversations he seemed to understand. Willow often asked him for advice on what to make for dinner or what movie to watch that night. She smiled at the memory of the time that she had spoken to the dog about what color to paint the kitchen and had even shown him swatches. He just stared at her as if reminding her that dogs saw color differently.

She adjusted in her seat so that she could analyze the financial documents that she had left on the porch table. She had to come to a decision that afternoon. She frowned.

"I guess this is the problem that most people and businesses have," she grumbled. "I want to do this, but I'm not sure I can afford it."

Telescope gave her a reassuring lick on the face.

"Thanks, Tele."

He did make her feel less grumpy, but it didn't make her decision any easier. She grabbed a blank piece of paper and began making a list of pros and cons. The groomer that most people brought their pets to in town was retiring, and this was providing an opportunity for her to expand her business. If she offered grooming services, then her place could become a "one-stop shop" for all your canine needs. She added these thoughts to the "pro" portion of her list and then wrote that it could attract customers that were both regular pet owners and breeders of the next Best in Show.

However, there was one major "con" on her list: "the price."

She had always considered adding a doggie spa section to her business but wasn't planning on doing it right away. After hiring her employees, which she admitted she needed, to help with the business she already had, it didn't leave much room for any additional renovations. However, if she wanted to capitalize on the groomer's retirement, she would have to act fast, and she'd need to begin the renovations ASAP.

"I guess it comes down to this," she said, tapping her pencil on her list. "In order to build the spa, I need money to do it."

Telescope just blinked as if what she said was too obvious to react to. Willow chuckled. She supposed it did sound as if she had suggested a dog dig up his bone before he had a chance to chew on it.

"What I mean is that I'd need to find a source for this money. But I do have an idea about that."

She sat pondering for a few more moments and then shrugged. She wasn't accomplishing much just sitting there. Her thoughts were running in circles, like a dog chasing his tail.

"What do you think?" she asked her furry friend.

Telescope jumped off the chair. He lay down on the ground and then rolled from side to side. He sat up and made a little yip.

"I'm sorry you have to play charades for me to understand while I get to ramble aloud."

He started running around the porch.

"Do you want to go through the obstacle course? Is that it?"

By way of an answer, he bounded towards the doggie gym. Willow collected her papers into a pile and placed her mug on them so they wouldn't blow away while she was gone. She followed after the dog, figuring enough time had passed that it wouldn't seem like she was checking up on the trainers needlessly.

Telescope ran past the outdoor obstacle course and doghouses and headed to the door that led to the indoor area. Willow was glad. Even though the day had ended up being beautiful, there had been a chance of rain in the forecast. The other owners and trainers had opted to play indoors because no one wanted to cause the "wet dog smell" if it could be helped. Willow wanted to see how the other canines were enjoying their playtime as well as allowing Telescope to have some fun too.

As soon as she entered, one of her trainers ran up to her. Willow didn't know how Shelly had so much energy, but she always seemed to be as excitable as a border collie. That could also be an apt description because Willow had seen her round up the dogs before.

"How was free play?" Willow asked.

Telescope appeared by her feet, and Shelly greeted him by petting his chin before addressing her boss.

"A small scuffle between a confused lab and a miniature pinscher that didn't know he was mini, but we took care of it quickly," she said. "Also, we've almost convinced Mr. Wenderson that you'll be able to handle training his Great Dane how to heel. He was concerned because he thinks the dog is bigger than you are."

"Ha. Ha," Willow said. Her short stature always seemed to be a joke with people who had larger breeds. "I'll talk to him and remind him how important early training is with the larger breeds."

She looked around the room to see who was still there. A woman who was wearing pearls even though she was at the dog gym was trying to convince her Yorkshire terrier to walk through a tube and meet her on the other end.

"Any news on Linda?" Willow asked, trying to be subtle as she gestured towards the woman with the stationary Yorkshire.

Linda was a new customer, but Willow was suspicious that she was actually there as a secret shopper. Willow knew that Linda had a reputation as a whistleblower at city hall as well as being a member of city council. Willow couldn't help wondering if she was investigating whether a gym for dogs was a scam.

Willow admitted that it was possible that Linda really did want to train her dog but based on how she rewarded the small pooch for sitting still even when she asked her to run, Willow thought it was unlikely. Either way, she would offer Linda the best services that her gym had to offer, just like she did every other customer.

Shelly shrugged. "She said that she wanted to work with her dog alone. That could be because she's overprotective or because she wants to do some snooping."

"I'll go talk to her."

Willow headed over to Linda and greeted her with a wave. Telescope followed and wagged his tail.

"I hope you're both enjoying your time here today," Willow said politely.

"I suppose so," Linda responded with a bit of disdain.

Telescope couldn't seem to contain himself anymore and headed towards the nearest obstacle to illustrate his skills. He ran through the tube quickly and then returned to them.

"Show off," Linda muttered. "My poor Pattie might be able to do that too. But you know that she's still recovering from all that surgery last year. She still gets tired. And she doesn't feel the need to prance around like some other dogs."

Instead of responding, Willow snapped her fingers at Telescope and pointed. He began heading through the tube again, but this time he went slower. Pattie slowly ventured inside the tube and followed him to the other end.

Linda looked duly impressed but directed all this attention towards her puppy. She picked up the dog and smoothed her long hair back affectionately.

While Willow thought the pup did deserve praise, she couldn't help thinking that she and Telescope deserved some of the credit too. Would Linda consider their help if she really did write a secret shopper review about her gym?

Willow was allowing her mind to wander about whether there was anything at her gym that could cause a negative write-up when Linda finally directed her attention back towards her.

"I suppose there are some perks to coming here instead of just training at home."

"Glad to hear you say that," Willow said. She beamed, accepting that this was actually high praise from her. "If you need anything, please let us know."

Then, Willow headed over to Telescope's favorite section of the obstacle course. She had done enough small talk and wanted to focus on the animals. She'd always felt that she understood canines better than people and was happy that most of the time she was able to deal exclusively with them.

She cheered for Telescope as he ran through a line of upright sticks, weaving left and right between them. He padded over to her when he was finished, and she gave him a full body rub.

It seemed like the gym was starting to wind down for the day as the designated hours for free play were drawing to a close.

A slight frown crossed Willow's face. There was one dog that she'd been hoping to see. She thought the dog was very skilled and training her just might provide Willow with an opportunity to build that doggie spa.

She ran one more obstacle with Telescope and then realized that the dog she had been hoping to see, along with her owner, had entered the gym.

Lady Valkyrie was a beautiful Irish setter with lush red hair and the perfect gait. Her owner, Terry Gib, had dyed her hair to match her dog's and had piled it on her head.

Terry smiled as she joined Willow. "I know I've told you this before, but I think your dog runs this course fantastically."

"He's pretty amazing," Willow replied. "He even saved my life once. Literally, that is. Metaphorically, he probably does it every day."

Terry placed a hand on Lady Valkyrie's head. "I understand that."

"I saw you here earlier, and I was afraid I missed you," Willow said, working up the courage to ask the question that she'd been thinking about all day.

"I needed to grab something from my car," Terry said with a laugh. "There are so many dog treats around here that it made me hungry, and I needed a granola bar."

Willow chuckled along and then said, "Have you thought any more about the Field Club Championship?"

Willow remembered every word that she had said about the championship because she had been practicing it before she spoke to Terry. She told her how Lady Valkyrie had all the makings of a true champion show dog and how, with proper training, she could win the Field Club competition. The dog show offered big prize money and an advertising campaign for a major dog food brand. Willow had done well at this competition in the past and was sure that she could succeed with Lady Valkyrie.

"You know that I don't want to rush into anything," Terry said, biting her lip.

Willow nodded. That was why she hadn't pressed the matter before. Terry had been in town a few days, and it was clear that she liked working with Willow. However, would this translate into letting her take over Lady Valkyrie's training?

If Willow's charge won the Field Club Championship, the percentage of the prize money she would receive would solve her current worries about expanding her business to include the spa. It could also lead to a big boom in customers.

"I completely understand," Willow said. "But tomorrow is the deadline to enter the competition."

"Tell you what," Terry said, "why don't I sleep on it? And I'll give you an answer in the morning? And we can continue from there?"

"Why don't the two of you come by here? We'll have an

early morning training session, and you can tell me what you decided."

"That sounds lovely," Terry said.

Then, Terry led Lady Valkyrie away to enjoy running a few more obstacles in the gym.

"I guess we'll find out tomorrow," Willow said, looking down at her dog.

She was nervous and excited but tried to will herself to remain calm. Even if Terry said no, her life was still relatively good. And as long as Willow didn't come across any other dead bodies, she would be happy.

2

Willow had never been much of a morning person, but she had been trying to improve her mood on the occasions that she needed to rise early. She reminded herself that getting to train a winning show dog was well worth it and ended up humming as she made breakfast.

Telescope always seemed ready for adventure, at her side, no matter the time of day. After she rewarded him for his loyalty with a few pieces of bacon, they headed to the obstacle course. Telescope was trying to show off, but Willow was distracted.

"I'm sorry, boy," she said. "But there could be a lot riding on this."

He grudgingly stopped running around and sat next to her.

Willow told him he was her best friend as they waited for Terry to arrive.

Finally, Terry's car pulled up to the house, and Willow reminded herself to play it cool. If the answer was no, she wouldn't curl up into a ball. If the answer was yes, she wouldn't jump up and down like a child. She needed to appear professional.

Terry emerged from the car, beaming, and Willow hoped this was a good sign. Terry opened the door for her dog, and Lady Valkyrie stepped out, shaking her head and letting her hair blow around her like a supermodel.

Willow touched her own dark hair for a moment, wondering how much better the dog's looked than hers. Then, she dismissed the thought. She was more interested in other matters.

Willow greeted Terry and her dog, and Terry did the same. She bit her lip and refrained from yelling, "What did you decide?"

"Thank you for being so patient with us," Terry said.

"No worries. Lady Valkyrie is worth it. And I don't feel like you've been stringing me along. I obviously hope that you'll choose to compete, but you told me all along how you didn't plan on rushing into this."

"You know that Lady Valkyrie had stepped on a nail a while back and even though she seems to have recovered fully from it, I didn't want to push her."

Willow nodded.

"I wanted to make sure that she was ready and, really, I'm not on any time schedule to begin competitions," Terry said.

"Of course," Willow said. She began thinking up the proper things to say to cover her disappointment.

"However," Terry continued. "I realized that she is ready now, and since I have such a willing trainer to help her go all the way – well, why not go for it?"

"Are you saying what I think you're saying?"

"We're going to enter the competition," Terry said. "And I think we're going to win it too."

Even though she had promised herself that she wouldn't, Willow jumped for joy. She collected herself and shook Terry's hand.

"I think we're going to do marvelously," Willow said in her most professional tone. "Why don't we do a few of the obstacles with Lady Valkyrie and then fill out the forms? We can finish the training session after her entrance is official."

Terry agreed, and Willow led Lady Valkyrie to the beginning of the course. The Field Club Championship would test her agility and poise as well as her ability to listen to commands.

Willow led her over some hurdles and was pleased by how the dog seemed to fly over them. She made quick work of the pyramids and raced around the cones. Her final trick was to race through the tube. She emerged looking victorious.

Willow was ecstatic. Training this dog wouldn't feel like jumping through hoops because Lady Valkyrie was so naturally skilled. Willow would just need to introduce the dog to new challenges that she had never faced before, prepare her for the competitive environment that was jammed with people and animals, and make sure that the dog didn't lose focus during a race.

Terry clapped her hands. The look on her face told Willow that she really did believe that they could win. Telescope was looking less enthusiastic.

"Sorry, boy, but this is my job," Willow whispered to him. "And I promise you can show off later when Wednesday comes over."

"Let's fill out the paperwork!" Terry said. "I can't wait to make Lady Valkyrie's entrance official."

Willow led the way from the gym towards her house where her office was. Telescope and Lady Valkyrie were running around happily, keeping pace with them.

"It's a beautiful day, isn't it?" Terry asked, taking in a deep breath of fresh air as they walked across the yard.

"It is," Willow said, pausing as they reached her porch. "And you seem very happy today."

"Part of it is because of my excitement for Lady Valkyrie's competition," Terry said. "But I admit there's another reason too."

"What's that?"

"Well, it's a very long story overall. But the quick version is that I finally had a breakthrough with an old friend. We've been estranged. But we cleared the air, and I think things are going to be much better now. We're not quite there yet, but we're on the road to being right."

"I'm glad to hear that," Willow said with a smile.

"It makes me feel like there is potential in the air."

"I know that feeling," Willow said, though hers was about training champions and building a spa.

"I've even decided I'm going to start dating again too," Terry said. "I know that seems like a lot of decisions to make in one night but airing my piece really did make me feel like I could move forward in all aspects of my life."

Willow took a step closer to the woman. Terry seemed to want to talk, and it would be rude not to engage. "I've been thinking about jumping back into the dating scene too."

"I had a pretty bad breakup last year, and I'd been focusing on my dogs in order to ignore it. But I'm ready to move on now."

Willow nodded. "I went through a bad divorce. I don't know if there ever really is a good divorce, but mine was *bad*. He kept my last business too, but I seem to be overcoming that, and I'm hoping to meet someone nice."

"And," Terry said conspiratorially, "someone really cute."

"What are you two whispering about?" a male voice asked.

Terry looked surprised, but Willow just grinned. She was used to her contractor, Griffin, appearing from around the corner now. She did look down at Telescope and tease him though. "I thought you were supposed to be a watchdog."

Telescope ignored her and ran over to greet Griffin who promptly started petting him in the right spots.

"I think you've met Griffin Maynard before," Willow said to Terry. "He's my contractor who brought the crumbling dog run I inherited back to life."

"Of course," Terry said.

Griffin rose back to his feet and shook her hand. Willow noticed the slight embarrassment in his vivid blue eyes that she always saw when he was caught playing with a dog instead of what he thought he should be doing.

"I just came to pick up some of my tools," he said.

"Are you still working on the dog gym?" Terry asked. "It looks perfect to me."

"The dog gym is done except for some touch ups in the storage area," Willow explained. "But the house isn't completely done yet."

Griffin nodded. "Just a few odd jobs left to finish up. She's letting me work on a small project for my next-door neighbor today, but I'll be back tomorrow."

"Your tools are right inside," Willow said, walking to the door. "I set them here while I was making breakfast so that they were easy to find."

"I'm surprised you could make breakfast and gather tools," he teased. "You're not normally functional in the morning."

"I function," she replied. "Maybe not a full speed, but I function."

"Should I be worried that there are scrambled eggs mixed in my toolbox?"

Willow laughed and gave him a playful push towards the tools. "See for yourself."

He examined the contents. "No eggs. No bacon. No cereal. All the tools I asked for. It looks like you did all right. I think you even learned what a lug wrench is."

"I always knew what a lug wrench was," she said. "I just liked calling you a big lug."

"Well, give me a call when you've finished your training for the day," he said, as he closed up the toolbox and grabbed the power saw next to it. "We'll discuss the plan of attack for the final steps."

"Sure," Willow said. "But I might have a new project for you too. I'll keep you posted."

He smiled broadly. In fact, Willow thought he seemed a little too happy by this news. He said goodbye to Terry and the dogs, and Willow could have sworn she heard him whistling as he walked away.

She returned to Terry who had an eyebrow raised suggestively. "And, perhaps, is this the reason you're willing to date again?"

"Griffin is just my contractor," Willow said, hoping it sounded true.

"You two seem pretty close.".

Willow felt her cheeks blush but shook her head definitively. "I like to keep my business and personal life separate. And Griffin is business."

"Your loss," Terry said with a sly smile..

Willow laughed. She was glad that she was becoming so friendly with Lady Valkyrie's owner. That would be important as the competition neared.

Telescope barked, and Willow thanked him.

"He must be announcing our next guest's arrival because I teased him about Griffin," she explained.

"He can really understand it when you say things like that?" Terry asked.

"He seems to," Willow said, and Telescope wagged his tail. "And that was his friendly announcement bark. It's probably my sister. She was supposed to come over later today, but she tends to arrive either fashionably late or fashionably early."

"I didn't know that was a thing."

"I didn't either," Willow agreed. "Until Wednesday appeared three hours early for our brunch date so I could help her decide what to wear. And of course, she chose the opposite of what I said."

"Willow!"

She turned and saw her little sister racing to hug her. Willow often felt tiny compared to her nearly six-foot tall, gorgeous blond sister, but when she was wrapped up in a bear hug, she felt even smaller.

When she finally released her, Wednesday said, "Wills, I have the best news! Guess."

"You won the lottery?"

"No. Why is that always your guess?" Wednesday said with an overly dramatic sigh. "I have a better chance of getting struck by lightning than winning the lottery."

"But that wouldn't be good news," Willow pointed out.

"Okay, fine. You're never going to guess."

Willow smiled. This was one of the techniques she used to get her sister to the point faster. Sometimes it worked and sometimes it didn't.

"I'll just tell you," Wednesday continued. Excitement was practically radiating off of her and Willow was eager to learn what was causing it. "I've been selected for a 'Week in My Life' feature for *Clickable ConTENt.*"

"What's that?" Terry asked.

Willow was glad that Terry asked because she wasn't completely certain herself.

"It's a major online and social media company. They have articles on basically everything. Everyone reads it. They have stories that you can't help but click on."

"That's wonderful that they picked you then," Willow said.

Telescope yipped excitedly.

"The person they were going to use had to back out," Wednesday explained. "Normally, they schedule people months out, so they needed to find somebody to fill in. They chose me because I'm fun and flirty and gained a ton of followers after my successful makeup campaign."

"What does a feature like that entail?" Terry asked.

"Just what it sounds like," Wednesday said. "I'll take pictures and videos and post about what it's like to be me in a typical week. Of course, I will try and splash it up a little bit. Make sure everything is exciting and clickable."

"We have some clickable news too," Willow said, trying not to feel ridiculous when she said it.

"What?"

"I'm going to train Lady Valkyrie to compete in the Field Club Championship show."

"And we're both going to start dating again," Terry added.

"Interesting," Wednesday said with a knowing smile.

Willow tried to steer the conversation back to something she was comfortable with, and said, "You're welcome to visit her and post some pictures of the dogs. The internet loves animals."

"True. And I appreciate it. I'm going to be running around, trying to figure out the best things to do this week, because it starts so soon. Monday! I want to be captivating and..." She trailed off as a look of horror came across her face.

"What is it?" Willow asked, hurrying towards her.

"This is the worst week of my life to follow a 'Week in My Life.'"

"Why?"

"It's review week at the station. I'm going to be tied to my police secretary desk doing boring paperwork. Who's going to want to follow that?"

"I'm sure you'll still look cute doing it," Willow said.

"I won't be able to brush it off either because, you know, it's the police station. Paperwork is important. And I need to write up a bio for Dad, so I want that to sound good."

Wednesday sat on the porch steps and frowned. The good mood was dissipating, but Willow was determined not to see it die.

"No," Willow said, confidently. "It won't be boring. You'll do your job and come up with exciting content this week. I know you can. Terry was right before when she said that it felt like it was time to move forward. And we're all going to move forward."

Wednesday returned to her feet. The three women gathered together, allowing themselves to be enthusiastic. The animals danced around their feet.

"Lady Valkyrie is going to compete and be amazing. I'm going to make sure of it. Wednesday, you're going to make this the best week of your life in all aspects. And Terry, you and I are going to find nice dates."

"I feel like we should all put our hands in the center and yell, *go, team*," Wednesday said.

"I feel like we should get to work," Willow said. "We've got a lot to do!"

3

"Very funny," Griffin said. He tried to keep a straight face, but the mirth was evident in his eyes.

"I thought it was," Willow said with a smile. She set the bacon-wrapped screwdriver on the counter, proud of the joke she had come up with based on their last interaction.

She poured them both a cup of coffee the way they liked it, and they both took a sip. Telescope was chomping on his breakfast in the corner while the humans talked. This was the easy routine that they had fallen into since construction got underway. Griffin would visit her kitchen, they would chat, and then he would begin building.

"That's exciting about Lady Valkyrie," he said, focusing on the other news that she had told him. "Do you really think she could go all the way?"

"I do," Willow said, nodding. "She's a perfect specimen of Irish setter, and she makes the obstacle course look easy."

"Tell me a little more about this dog show," he said, setting down this coffee. "Because I thought in most shows, dogs just walked around in a big circle, and the judges touched them one at a time."

Willow chuckled at this not entirely inaccurate description of a dog show. "Shows that focus on breeds often do that, but the Field Club Championship is more of an athletic competition. They have to complete obstacle courses as part of their judging."

"Like the Olympics but for dogs?" Griffin asked.

"That's not a bad way of looking at it," she said.

She checked that Telescope was still set with his food while Griffin tapped his mug. Finally, he said, "I watched that movie you recommended the other day."

Willow grinned. She had suggested an action comedy that she came across on Netflix. She liked all the quips that the characters came up with and was sure he would too. She also figured that Griffin would admire the architecture of the historic buildings – even if most of them did end up exploding in the film.

"Well, Tele suggested I watch it," Willow said, giving credit where it was due. "I was being indecisive and had him point a paw at the title I should pick."

Griffin nodded. He looked at the ground and then met her eyes. "Maybe we should watch one together sometime?"

Willow paused. That sounded an awful lot like he was asking her out on a date. No. That couldn't be it. She must have been misreading the situation. His offer was just part of comradery they shared after being involved in a murder investigation and rebuilding a house.

"I don't know," Willow said, trying to deflect the awkward feelings she felt. "Could Tele pick out another movie as good?"

The dog looked up from his food and tilted his head.

"Maybe," Griffin said, picking up his mug again and hiding behind it for a moment to take a sip. "But I have been thinking about how the construction is almost done. And about how I'm going to miss talking to you like this. I've really enjoyed chatting with you before I got to work."

"I'm glad you said that," Willow said, cheerfully. "Remember how I said that I might have another project for you?"

"Yeah," he responded, though this time he looked unsure instead of happy.

"I've been thinking about adding a doggie spa to the place. It could be attached to my office here on the first floor, and we could adapt the bathroom."

"This is the project you were talking about?" he asked.

Willow nodded. "The main Pineview groomer is retiring, and this is a prime opportunity for me to expand my business. Dogs can work out and then be washed to smell nice. That's a great idea, isn't it?"

"I know you talked about this before and said you possibly wanted to do it someday. I didn't think you planned on doing it so soon."

"I didn't know there would be a need for a new groomer in Pineview," Willow said. "But if I don't jump on it now, then the need will be filled."

Griffin began pacing around the kitchen with his cup in hand. "How do I ask this delicately?"

"You want to ask about the money?" Willow said with a smile.

"Yeah," Griffin said, stopping and turning to face her. "I thought you had just enough money to do the training areas and a few rooms of your house. I know there were even a few household projects that you decided to put on hold because you wanted to save money."

"And I decided that all my bedroom and guest room need are a coat of paint each," Willow said. "I'm not losing out there. I don't really need to show off my master bedroom."

Why did she add that part at the end? Griffin didn't need to know that part. Feeling insecure, she covered it up with a laugh.

"But how are you going to pay for the spa?" He added quickly, "Believe me, if I could do the work for free, I would. You did make sure that I wasn't arrested for murder."

"Griffin," Willow said, moving closer, "I would never ask you to do work for free. You're my contractor. I'm supposed to pay you."

"But we are a little more…" he said, moving his hands as he spoke. "I mean… we are friends."

Willow wasn't quite sure what to make of his pauses. She took a step away, but repeated, "I would never ask you to work for free."

"Well, then, where is the money coming from?" he asked, crossing his arms.

"Lady Valkyrie," Willow explained. "If she wins the championship, there's prize money and an advertising contract. I'd get a percentage of it, and it would more than pay for the renovations."

"Oh," was all he said.

"I'm not saying we should break ground right away. The championship isn't that far off. But I'd like to keep you on for this new project."

Griffin nodded.

"What's wrong?"

"I'm just surprised," he said.

Willow sensed there was more to the story and was about to ask him to elaborate. She trusted his opinion about the construction, and he knew more about Pineview than she did sometimes. She had been gone for several years before she moved back after her divorce and planned to do things on her own terms this time. Maybe Griffin knew something about the groomer that she didn't. Maybe he knew about the issues involved in installing the tub necessary for bathing both Great Danes and Chihuahuas.

She was about to question him when Telescope barked. A moment later her doorbell rang.

"We'll talk about this in a minute," Willow said.

Griffin just nodded. She rolled her eyes when she was sure he couldn't see her. She didn't like when he became secretive.

She opened the door and saw Terry, but she was so unlike the happy Terry from the day before. Willow barely recognized her. She was no longer smiling and glowing with positivity. Her red hair was falling out of her bun, and she looked like she might pass out.

Telescope ran to the door and sat next to Willow's feet. She frowned. It was much earlier than Terry was supposed to arrive for training, and, in fact, it was an hour before the dog gym was supposed to open. Terry looked so upset that Willow was sure that something terrible had happened.

She waited for Terry to speak and when she didn't, Willow asked, "Terry, what's wrong? Is it Lady Valkyrie?"

"Lady Valkyrie?" Terry repeated. "No. She seemed to take it better than I did."

"Take what?"

"Seeing her like that."

"Who?" Willow asked. She didn't understand any of this. "Where is Lady Valkyrie?"

"She's in my room," Terry said. "I thought she should rest. But I couldn't stay still. I needed to move. I decided to go for a walk. I know the irony – another walk. But I had to do something."

"I'm glad Lady Valkyrie is safe," Willow said. "But I'm not really sure what else you're telling me."

"Of course, Lady Valkyrie is safe," Terry said. "I don't know about Polly, though. I should have asked about Polly. That's what I should have done. I should have checked on Polly instead of coming here. I'm not sure what I was thinking."

Griffin joined her in the entryway.

"Who is Polly?" he asked.

"I don't know," Willow said. "We haven't gotten that far."

Terry leaned against the doorframe. Willow placed an arm on her shoulder.

"Terry, who is Polly?" she asked gently.

"Kaitlin's dog."

"And Kaitlin is…?" Griffin said, trailing off to allow her to answer.

They were both surprised by Terry's answer to the pause. "Dead."

"Pardon?" Willow asked.

"Kaitlin is dead," Terry said. When the words were out of her mouth, there was finality to it. She seemed to look even sadder.

"That does sound terrible, and we're sorry that her death affects you so," Griffin said. "But, now, who is Kaitlin?"

"The owner of the B&B I was staying at," Terry explained. "Kaitlin Janes. She died this morning."

"Oh no," Willow said. "Is there something we can do?"

"There might be," she said. "You see, I saw her die."

Willow and Griffin exchanged a look. Willow could sense that Griffin had no more idea where this conversation was going than she did, but she thought he agreed that it was starting to sound more and more creepy.

"You saw Kaitlin die?" Willow asked.

"Lady Valkyrie and I were walking. It's our usual morning route now. It's on Main Street. There are lots of other dog walkers at that time. I saw Kaitlin ahead of us with Polly. I was debating whether I should call out to her or not. But then she started stumbling. She fell over and someone caught her. I was too distracted to see who. Everyone on the street ran over to her, but there was nothing we could do. When I reached her, I saw her nose was bleeding. And then... she died."

Willow shuddered. She didn't want to imagine seeing someone that she knew die right in front of her.

"An ambulance was called, and they took her away. They told us to leave, and I took Lady Valkyrie back to our room. I didn't know what to do. I don't know many people in town. But then I realized that I do know you," Terry said. She stopped leaning on the doorframe and stood up straight. "And I remembered hearing about how you helped with a case before and caught a killer."

"I wish people would stop talking about that," Willow murmured.

"I thought you could maybe help again."

Willow shifted uncomfortably. "How?"

34

"I want you to help me track down Kaitlin's old boyfriend, Jack. Jack Grim. We have to find him."

"Terry," Willow said, trying to be firm but reassuring. "I think it's best if the police handle notifying the friends and family about her death. They have professionals who know how to do that sort of thing."

"Inform him of the death?" Terry said. "He knows about it all right."

"I don't understand," Willow said.

"Me neither," Griffin muttered under his breath.

"I think Jack Grim killed her," Terry said, grabbing Willow's shoulders. "I want you to catch her killer."

4

"Drink this," Willow said, forcing a cup of coffee into Terry's hand. She had brought the frazzled woman into her kitchen and was trying to figure out a way to get the full story out of her. She had her sit on one of the stools.

Terry took a sip and then placed the mug on the island counter. Telescope touched her leg with his front paw, and Griffin deposited the dog into her lap. Petting the dog's head seemed to calm her.

Willow was glad because as she looked around her kitchen, she didn't see much to offer the woman to soothe her. She sat on a stool opposite from Terry and decided to start from the beginning.

"Why do you think Kaitlin was murdered?" Willow asked.

Terry continued rubbing Tele's fur and took a deep breath.

"I know Kaitlin."

"Right," Griffin said. "You said that she was the lady who owned the B&B."

"I've heard of her," Willow said as she put things together. "She's got the place you want to stay at if you're traveling to Pineview with a dog. It's very accommodating and canine friendly."

"One of the only places that is," Terry said. "Which was why I had to stay there, despite my history with Kaitlin. And I have to admit that it wasn't a great one. We used to be friends, but then we had a big falling out. Actually, she was the person I was referring to when I said that I finally cleared the air with someone. I thought things were finally going to improve between us, but now we won't have the chance to move forward."

Willow placed her hand on the hand that Terry wasn't using to pet the dog. She hoped it was comforting. She knew that she was much better at comforting her furry companions than human ones.

"That sounds very upsetting," Willow said. "And I can see why you'd want to believe there was a reason that she was taken from you that didn't seem so random. But what you described before sounds like an illness."

Griffin nodded. "Her stumbling and nosebleed could have been an aneurysm."

"No. It wasn't," Terry said. "That's what I meant when I said I knew Kaitlin. I knew all about her. We used to be as close as two people could be. I know all her medical history, and she didn't have any conditions that would lead to this."

"But some time has passed?" Griffin suggested. "Maybe it changed?"

"And sometimes people don't like discussing their illnesses with others," Willow said. "Or they don't know that they have a condition until it's too late."

"Kaitlin didn't die of natural causes," Terry said, shaking her head. "I know it."

Willow bit her lip. "It sounds as if the EMTs believes she did."

Some color returned to Terry's face, but it seemed to come from anger. "If you could have seen her like that, you'd agree with me. You'd know that this wasn't some sort of illness."

Willow looked at Griffin. It seemed as if Terry wasn't accepting logic anymore, and Willow didn't know what else to offer her. Griffin looked back helplessly and shrugged. It seemed he didn't know what to do either.

Telescope cuddled closer to Terry, and she accepted the affection. Then, something seemed to come over her. She gave Telescope a final pat on the head, then handed him back to Willow.

Confused by what was happening, Willow hugged her dog close to her chest. Terry was getting to her feet, and Willow followed suit, still holding Tele.

"You're not going to track down Jack for me?" she asked.

"I think this is something for the police to handle," said Willow. "You might be misled by grief."

"I'm thinking very clearly," Terry said, sounding more like herself. She began fixing her hair as she continued. "I'm almost certain that Jack killed Kaitlin, and I need to find him. I'll just have to put training Lady Valkyrie on hold until I can settle this."

"Hold on just a minute," Willow said, holding out a palm to indicate stop while still balancing her dog. "Let's not do anything rash."

"I understand why you're hesitant to believe me," Terry said, as she finished her hair. "But I know it's true, and I have to do something about it. I owe it to Kaitlin."

Willow set Telescope on the floor to have full use of her hands. He sat on the spot she placed him, eager to continue watching the action. Griffin looked like he wanted to escape the conversation but was making no moves to leave Willow alone.

"Why do you think that Jack Grim had something to do with her death?" Willow asked.

"Do you recognize the name at all?" Terry asked. "Jack Grim?"

Willow thought about it and frowned. "Now that you mention it, it does sound familiar."

"He was on a reality TV show and has made other guest appearances. He wrote a book, and he has a podcast that's apparently pretty big right now."

"What's he famous for?" Willow asked.

"Being single," Terry said wryly.

"But he was Kaitlin's ex-boyfriend?" Willow asked.

"That's right. And he's made a career of being a bachelor. He makes his money telling people how to be successful on dates, but he can't appear to be tied down. It wouldn't be good for his image."

"But, they were exes, right? So, that shouldn't affect his image now," Willow pointed out.

"You don't know Jack. I did. I saw him and Kaitlin together, and it wasn't good. He is capable of this. And especially after speaking to Kaitlin again, I know it could be true. And," Terry said as if this were the nail in the coffin, "I saw him the other day. He's in town."

"Okay. That does make things seem more suspicious," Willow admitted.

"I don't know," Griffin said, speaking up. "Being a secret ex-boyfriend isn't a crime."

Both women glared at him. He held his hands up in defeat.

"Forget it," he said and headed over to the coffee maker to brew a fresh pot.

Willow looked at Terry. She seemed so sure about Jack's guilt. Willow wasn't anxious to get involved in another investigation, especially when a crime might not even have occurred.

On the other hand, she didn't want to lose the opportunity to compete with Lady Valkyrie because Terry was imagining

40

murders. She needed to keep her on track, or they would lose the championship.

She took a few steps around the kitchen, trying to organize her thoughts and reconcile these opposing forces. An idea occurred to her, and she spun around to face Terry.

"You said Jack tells people how to be good dates?"

"That's right. He's a dating coach as well as a bachelor personality."

"Why don't I call him and set up an appointment?" Willow suggested. "That way I can question him about Kaitlin but not seem obvious about it. And I might be able to set your mind at ease."

"I don't know about this," Griffin said, looking up from the coffee grounds.

"No. It's a great idea," Terry said. "I'm sure he'd remember me, but he's never seen you before. He wouldn't know that you were searching for evidence to prove he's a killer."

"Well, looking to see if he's involved," Willow amended. "And who knows? Maybe I'll actually get some good advice."

"That's true. We might need it," Terry said. "Though I'm not sure I'd trust it from him."

Griffin abandoned the coffee and moved closer to the group.

"You're actually seeking dating advice?" he asked.

"Yeah," Willow said, trying to shrug it off as if it weren't a big deal. "I mean, Terry and I had been talking about getting back in the dating saddle yesterday. And I guess I'm a bit out of practice, so it might be something that I could get advice on."

"I could give some advice," Griffin said. "Dating isn't something you need to practice. You find somebody that you like, and you ask her if she'd like to see a movie. You just need to be yourself, and then you see how things play out."

"Well, finding the somebody that you like can be the tricky part," Willow said.

"It could be someone right under your nose," Griffin countered.

She purposely avoided eye contact with him. Not wanting to give a real answer to that suggestion, she decided to deflect and opted for a joke. "I'm so short, the only one under my nose is Tele. And I pictured the man of my dreams having better breath."

Griffin didn't laugh. He looked serious. "You just need to take a risk."

"And she is," Terry said, stepping forward. "She's going to take a risk by talking to a killer for me."

Willow was grateful for the interruption. She grabbed her laptop from the other room and began searching for Jack Grim online. She found his website and a number to call.

"Here I go," Willow said as she punched the number into her phone. She turned to Terry. "Of course, he might be very busy. He is a famous dating coach, right? It might be a little while before he can see me. But I promise I will talk to him and get this sorted out."

She pressed the call button and waited as it rang. Terry was looking nervous, and Griffin was looking grumpy. Willow was nonchalant. She felt like she had figured out the perfect way to settle the situation. Jack would surely be too busy to see her right away. He was a famous and busy man. She would make an appointment to see him, and the waiting period would give Terry some time to calm down.

If Terry did decide that she'd been wrong to make those accusations when she was so upset, maybe she could accept that Kaitlin's death might have been due to an illness. Willow could always cancel the appointment. If it was no longer part of an investigation, she could decide whether this was embarrassing or not.

Then a man on the other end of the line spoke up. "Jack Grim, Dating Guru. What's up?"

"Hi. I'm Willow Wells." She could feel the eyes of the other people in the room upon her and tried not to react to his self-proclaimed title. "I was hoping to set up an appointment to go over some dating advice. You see, I've been out of the game for a long time."

"You in Pineview?"

"Yes."

"Let's meet for coffee in an hour."

"An hour?" Willow asked. Well, there went her plan to give Terry time to calm down.

"That's right. I had a cancellation, so I have an opening in an hour. Come on down to my office."

"Sure," Willow said, hoping she had hidden the disappointment in her voice.

She hung up the phone and Terry hugged her.

"You're meeting him in an hour? This is great news."

"I don't think you'll get any good advice though," Griffin said. "The best thing to do is just jump into the dating game."

"Ask him about Kaitlin and see how he reacts," Terry advised.

"You're sure you can't come with me?" Willow asked. She was hoping that the answer would still be no, but she'd rather know in advance.

"I can't. I think he would recognize me, and then he'll know that I've figured him out."

Willow nodded. "Well, I've got to go get ready," she said.

Maybe it would be good that the meeting was right away. She might be able to wrap it all up in an hour. All she had to do was meet with Jack Grim and feel him out, and then she could reassure Terry that he wasn't up to anything nefarious. But first, she needed to figure out what to wear.

5

"Hey, Wednesday, what does one wear to a meeting with a dating coach?" Willow asked. She held her cell phone up to her ear in one hand and an outfit she was sure she was going to reject in the other hand.

Terry had left to check that Lady Valkyrie was safe at their hotel room, and Griffin had gotten to work on the final projects around the house. Telescope had followed him off, and Willow was glad. She didn't like how loudly Griffin was hammering, and she felt he was protesting her meeting with Jack Grim.

"You're meeting a dating coach?" Wednesday asked. "That seems sudden and random. But it also sounds more exciting than the paperwork I've been filling out today."

"Well, it's not just for dating advice," Willow said and began explaining the situation.

"You had me at potential murderer," Wednesday said. "No. You had me at dating coach. Who am I kidding? You had me at – what should I wear? I'm coming over."

"What about work?"

"This is for my other job. The posts for my feature. I bet I could get a bunch of hits if I show myself spending time with a famous dating coach."

"You mean you're coming with me to talk to him too? Not just helping me with the outfit?"

"I bet I could cross-promote with him and get even more of an audience," Wednesday said excitedly. "And, of course, I would be there as your backup in case he really is a killer."

"I guess that is a good idea," Willow admitted.

"I'll be right there. Pick out a few potential outfits for me to choose from. Just make sure that maroon dress with the belt isn't one of them."

Willow looked at the maroon dress that she was holding and sighed.

"Call him to let him know that I'll be there too," Wednesday said. "Okay? I'm on my way. Bye!"

Willow hung up that call and redialed Jack Grim's number.

"Hi, this is Willow. We spoke a few minutes again."

"You better not be standing me up, baby. That's a big no-no."

"Not at all," she said. "I was just calling to say that I am going to bring my sister with me to the meeting."

"You're bringing your sister?" Willow could hear the disbelief dripping from his voice. "You do need help with your dating life. Good thing you're coming."

Willow could have argued with him and explained Wednesday's social media campaign idea, but instead, she just agreed and hung up. She threw the maroon dress onto a chair.

She was supposed to be busy training a show dog. How did her day end up like this?

Dressed in a Wednesday-approved business casual outfit, Willow entered Jack Grim's office with her sister at her side. She wasn't quite sure what she expected a dating guru's workplace to look like, but it was even more obnoxious that she thought it would be. Large posters of Jack Grim from his TV appearances and book jackets adorned the walls. Mixed in amid the décor were statues in various poses from the karma sutra.

Willow reminded herself that she was doing this for Lady Valkyrie. Then she adjusted her thoughts and added that she was also doing this for the deceased woman. If there was a chance that she really had been murdered, Willow had to do something about it.

"Sisters," Jack Grim said, entering the lobby.

"Hi. I'm Willow," she said, extending her hand to shake his.

Jack opted to kiss it instead and then reached for Wednesday's who accepted it with more good humor than Willow had.

"I must say, if I knew the two of you would be so lovely, I wouldn't have made a fuss at all."

"Did Willow not tell you what I wanted to do?" Wednesday asked, making a face at her sister without Jack seeing. Willow stuck her tongue out back at her and Jack happened to see that.

"What did you want to do?" he asked suggestively, then laughed as if he had told a great joke.

"I'm doing a 'Week in My Life' piece for *Clickable ConTENt*, and I was hoping that I could take some pictures of me supporting my sister in her search for love."

Jack seemed to give *Clickable ConTENt* the due that Wednesday thought it deserved. Willow noticed that he didn't have to ask what it was.

"I think we might be able to work something out," he said. "What did you have in mind?"

"I could plug your business in my posts, and you could tag me on your site? We could cross-promote each other and get more hits."

Jack nodded, and Willow felt her mind wandering as the two of them discussed their plans for the angle of the piece. Her attention snapped back when she heard her name.

"Maybe the advice you give Willow will be helpful to one of our followers," Wednesday said.

"I'm always game for a social media bump," he agreed.

"And if it's not helpful, at least it might be humorous."

Willow frowned.

"Her dating life is that bad?" Jack asked.

"It's not bad," Wednesday said. "It's nonexistent!"

"Hey," Willow said defensively. "I'm not that terrible at dating. I was married."

"And how did that turn out?" Jack asked. He rubbed his chin as if this was a very profound question.

"I never said anything bad about Benjamin while you were married," Wednesday said. "But now can I let loose?"

Willow also had some choice words to describe her ex. Benjamin had been controlling and manipulative. He had not been a partner in the true sense of the word. She resented how much time she had spent living up to his ideas of what she should be instead of being true to herself, and she hated that he had been able to keep her original dog training business in the divorce.

Still, she liked to think of the future and not focus on mistakes of the past.. In fact, the reason she had left Pineview originally and even met Benjamin had been due to a mistake.

However, she didn't plan on saying any of this to Jack Grim, and she hoped her sister wouldn't either. Wednesday must have interpreted the look on her face because she switched gears.

"Nah. Complaining about Benjamin would take hours. It's better if I tell you about her dates in high school."

"That was forever ago," Willow protested.

"As an outsider, how would you describe these dates?" Jack asked.

"I'd say that she pushed away all the people who would have made her happy, and instead she dated Eugene Filhop."

"Eugene was nice," Willow said.

Wednesday rolled her eyes. "Tell the truth. You were only dating him to spend time with his dog."

Willow opened her mouth to protest but then giggled. "He did have a really beautiful Weimaraner."

"I think I'm getting the picture here," Jack said. "But why don't we get some real pictures in a photo shoot? And then we'll get down to the consultation?"

Wednesday whipped out her phone in agreement. Willow tried to look happy as they staged some photos with Jack in front of a picture of himself. They took a few shots of her appearing thoughtful as he spoke to her and then took one of a group hug.

Afterwards, Jack led them into a side room where he said he usually conducted his meetings. It was set up like a restaurant with a table for two in the middle. This must be where some of the "practice dates" took place.

Jack smiled as Wednesday showed him her favorite pics, the ones she planned to post and said she would continue to take candid shots throughout. Willow hoped that the session would be fruitful enough to warrant a group hug after, but she wasn't feeling optimistic. Still, talking about her dating life might provide a segue for her to ask about his relationship with Kaitlin.

"So," Jack asked, settling into a seat and inviting Willow to sit across from him. "What are you looking for in a relationship?"

"Someone loyal and caring," she said, trying not feel as awkward as if she actually were on a first date. "And... acrobatic."

Wednesday stopped taking pictures and crossed her arms. "Are you just describing Tele, so you don't have to really answer the question?"

"No," Willow said, looking away. "Maybe."

"And Tele is?" Jack asked.

"Her dog," Wednesday said, blabbing.

"I'm sensing a theme with the canines here," Jack said.

"Wends, remember why we're really here?" Willow said, trying to convey her secret meaning. "You don't need to sell me out. And besides, it's not like you're always dating."

"I date all the time," Wednesday said. "I just haven't met anyone I like enough to introduce to you or Dad. I know that I'm multifaceted and want someone who can keep up with me. Besides that, I don't know exactly what else I'm looking for in a partner. But I enjoy going on dates and talking to attractive men, so they provide me with an opportunity to learn what I like."

"That sounds very self-aware," Jack said, praising her.

"Thanks," Wednesday said. "Selfie!"

She posed with Jack giving her the thumbs up. Willow considered what her sister had just said. She might as well answer some of these questions honestly and see what advice she got.

"Okay," Willow said, "I want to be in a relationship that feels natural and where I can be myself. I want to have fun with a guy and to be with someone who I can tease and who makes me laugh. He's got to love dogs. That's a deal breaker."

"Strong canine theme," Jack repeated in a mutter.

"And I want him to have his own thing and for me to have mine, but when we work on things together, we'd make a good team," Willow finished, impressed by how she'd opened up.

"You know who that sounds like?" Wednesday asked.

Willow saw the smug look on her face and groaned. "Don't say Griffin."

"But it does sound like Griffin," Wednesday protested.

"Who is Griffin?" Jack asked. "Another dog?"

"My contractor!"

"The guy she secretly likes," Wednesday said.

"No," Willow said. "I'm not going there again. I'm keeping my business and personal life separate. Griffin is part of my business life. He's the man who built my training facility and who will hopefully build my doggie spa, as well as any other projects that might creep up."

"But—" Wednesday began, but Willow cut her off.

"No buts," Willow said. "I learned from Benjamin. You need to keep your business separate from your love life."

Wednesday didn't offer a rebuttal. Instead, she focused on her phone and began posing for more pictures.

"Do you want my advice?" Jack asked.

"Sure," Willow said. "That's the reason I'm here."

"It seems that in your last major relationship you didn't feel like you were truly yourself. When you go on dates in the future, make sure that the suitors get to see the real you. Then, if all goes well, it will be based on truth. And you should be able to break the cycle of your last relationship."

"That's actually pretty good advice," Willow said, impressed. "The be yourself part is similar to what Griffin told me."

However, Willow's kindly feelings towards Jack Grim didn't last long. "Of course, in order to get to that first date, you're going to have to attract a man. And it so happens, I offer a class for just that. Flirting, winking, suggestion. We cover it all."

Willow barely stopped herself from rolling her eyes but then sensed an opening.

"I don't know," she said. "Are these classes really worth it? After all, you are a bachelor, aren't you? What do you know about being in a relationship?"

"A curse of the trade, baby," he said with a laugh. "But I

know all there is to know about attracting a mate and keeping one."

"But you don't have one yourself?"

"Nope. I'm enjoying the single life and dating lovely ladies too much."

"But there have been some exceptions to this rule?"

"Well, if someone really special were to come along, we might last for more than one night. But I'm not one to kiss and tell. Unless it's on TV," he joked.

"Who was that someone special?" Willow asked.

"Let's focus on you," he suggested.

"Was Kaitlin special?"

Jack blinked, but then immediately responded with, "Well, I've known a lot of Kaitlins through the years."

"Kaitlin Janes?" Willow said, keeping a close eye on him for a reaction. He remained cool. He just shook his head and laughed.

"You're trying to trick me into giving away some insider information, aren't you? I'm afraid that won't work."

"You won't talk about her at all?" Willow asked.

Jack looked towards the door, and she could tell if this had been a real date, that Jack would have asked for the check by now.

"I haven't admitted that I even know this woman you're talking about," he said.

"Oh," Willow said, leaning across the table. "So, her death

means nothing to you? The fact that she toppled over and died while walking her dog doesn't faze you?"

This got a physical reaction from Jack. He leaned onto the table to steady himself and turned pale.

"Kaitlin is dead?"

"So, you admit you know her?" Willow asked, a little more gently.

"Yeah. I guess I can tell you I knew her," he said. "And you did too? You want to find out why she's dead?"

"Something like that," Willow said.

Wednesday put her phone away and watched the exchange.

"If that's the case, the person you should be talking to is Terry Gib," Jack said.

"Terry?"

"That's right. I wouldn't put it past her to do something like this. Terry was cutthroat. Just look at what she was like when she and Kaitlin were in the beauty pageant circuit together. She was a cheat. And she might have just progressed to becoming a killer."

"You really think that Terry Gib could have killed her?" Wednesday asked.

"Yes," Jack said solemnly. He cleared his throat and stood up. "But if you'll excuse me, I have another client coming in. And this mama's boy needs some serious help."

Willow allowed herself to be ushered out the door.

Wednesday promised to tag him in her posts, and he agreed but less enthusiastically than before.

"That was weird," Willow said, as they walked towards the car.

"Which part?" Wednesday asked.

"Okay. All of that was weird," Willow admitted. "But I was referring to when he suggested that Terry could have killed Kaitlin."

"Because she's your client and a friend now?"

"Because he also assumed that Kaitlin had been murdered," Willow said. "I still think it's likely that she died because of an illness. So why do two people already suspect that she was murdered? Was it because she was young? Or it is something in her past that makes everyone think this?"

Wednesday shrugged. "Good questions."

Willow nodded and kept thinking. They were questions she would like to find answers to, and soon.

6

"It's not fair," Willow said.

Telescope made a snorting sound of agreement. They were both watching Lady Valkyrie fly over the last hurdles in the obstacle course, and he obviously wanted a chance to compete too. Willow ruffled his ears.

She supposed things weren't quite fair for him either. However, what she had been referring to was how training a competition-ready Irish setter now came with the caveat that she needed to look into a potential crime. Willow tried not to sigh. How could wanting to work with such a beautiful dog lead Willow into trouble?

She didn't want to dwell on Terry's request for her to solve a murder, but it felt like it was looming over her. After all, as far as she knew, Kaitlin Janes had died of natural causes. This sort of thing happened every day. It was sad, but it wasn't criminal. And it was far more likely that this was just a tragic death and not another homicide.

Either way, she didn't want to think about it. She wanted to focus on the training session and on her plans for preparing for the championship. Willow smiled as she went through the list of notions she had for the training schedule. She liked being able to focus on her time with the dogs. It was certainly less complicated than dating or murder.

She worked with Lady Valkyrie for the rest of the afternoon while Telescope alternated between watching them and entertaining himself with a rope toy. The Irish setter made her jumps look effortless, and she was sure to impress the judges.

As they finished up, Willow couldn't help but be glad that she had been able to train with Lady Valkyrie alone. She didn't want to face Terry for an extended period while she was still figuring out her feelings towards her. Willow had wanted to work with Terry, but now she had doubts. Was Terry keeping secrets from her? Did she have a dark past?

And what about Kaitlin? If multiple people thought that she had been murdered, she had to be involved in something that could warrant those accusations. What could it be?

Then, another thought entered her head. Should she go to her dad with these suspicions? He was the Chief of Police and valued her opinion, so he would be the prime person to inform about a crime. But all she really had to report right now were two people's suspicions, and they were both pointing fingers at one another.

She told Lady Valkyrie and Telescope to enjoy some free time, and the dogs began to frolic. Then she began to clean up the training area. It wasn't especially messy, but there were chew toys left around the room. As she put the items in their rightful places, she couldn't help thinking that she was glad that one problem was easy to tidy up.

Terry entered the gym and waved nervously. Willow responded with a plastic bone in her hand.

"Let me help," Terry said.

After greeting Lady Valkyrie, Terry gathered the toys off the floor. Willow watched her out of the corner of her eye. She couldn't stop herself from feeling a little suspicious. Was there some merit to what Jack Grim had said about her? How much did Willow really know about Terry anyway?

With two of them working, the doggie gym was soon clean. Then, Willow realized it was time to face the music. She was going to have to talk to Terry about what she had heard and, honestly, she was going to have to hear some good answers in response in order to keep working with the other woman.

"I appreciate you letting me train Lady Valkyrie privately today," Willow began.

"It's quite all right," Terry said. "I trust you."

"Thanks," Willow said as a response because she wasn't able to return that particular compliment. "It gave me some time to look at the few kinks that we have to work on before the competition. And it did give me some time to gather my thoughts about Jack Grim."

"I understand," Terry said. "You said that it wasn't obvious that he was involved, but you wanted to think about the interaction a little more before you told me all the details. And I can see where you're coming from. It's a big deal to accuse someone of murder."

Willow couldn't help saying, "Of course, it comes more easily for some people than others."

She kicked the artificial grass that they were on.

"Well, what's your conclusion now?" Terry asked.

Willow looked her in the eyes. "The truth is that I don't know what to think. The strange thing that I mentioned happening? It was that Jack accused you of her murder."

Terry pointed a finger towards herself as if she didn't believe it. "Me?"

"He didn't know that I knew you, and I never said that I thought she was murdered. Only that she died," said Willow, driving home the point. "But the first thing he said when he heard she was dead was that I should ask you about your involvement."

"I can't believe he'd say that about me."

"And that's not all he said. He mentioned cutthroat behavior and your time together in the pageant circuit."

The other woman just shook her head and muttered about the term cutthroat.

"Terry, I think you need to tell me the whole story."

She sighed and turned away. Lady Valkyrie must have sensed her master's distress. She ran to her and leaned against her leg. Terry placed a hand on the dog's head and nodded.

"I asked you to get involved, so it's not fair if I keep you in the dark."

Telescope ran to the group and sat next to the Irish setter, watching what was unfolding. Willow crossed her arms, waiting for the woman to continue.

"I still think Jack is involved. And I do have some more details I could share that would support this. But I suppose I should address what he said about me first."

"What did he mean about the beauty pageants?" Willow asked.

"Kaitlin and I used to work them together. She was my coach, and I used to excel in the pageants. My talent was singing, which always pleased the judges. I was in shape at the time. My natural hair color looked nice too," she said, playing with her hair. "But I like the way it complements Lady Valkyrie now."

"Did you win many competitions?"

"I did," Terry said. "But I suppose it wasn't all completely due to my talents and poise. Kaitlin and I were competitive, and she pushed me. We did a few things that weren't completely above board, but I never did anything outrageous. And I never cheated."

"But Kaitlin did?"

Terry nodded. "And I couldn't deal with that. I left the pageant world and tried to find another one," she said sadly. She knelt down and brushed her dog with her hand. "But I think I found it with Irish setters. They're so majestic but also loyal. And I can still be a part of competitions. But it doesn't have to be me on stage anymore. I've had enough of that."

"It sounds like Kaitlin was the cutthroat one and not you," Willow said, frowning.

"Which is another reason why I think Jack has to be involved," Terry said, returning to her feet. "If he was dating Kaitlin at the time, then he would know that it was her behavior at the semifinals that was so ruthless, and not mine. He must be trying to push the blame onto me to get away with what he did."

"His motive doesn't seem that strong to me though," Willow said. She counted on her fingers. "His relationship with her was a long time ago. Dating gurus should be allowed to be in relationships sometimes. He's single now, which is the image he wants. How does her death help him?"

Terry moved closer to Willow even though they were the only people in the room. She appeared to want this to remain confidential.

"I'm sorry that I didn't tell you this earlier, but I didn't want to betray a confidence. Even if it was to a dead woman."

Willow was intrigued. "Go on."

"I immediately thought of Jack as a suspect because of his on-again, off-again relationship with Kaitlin. They went on like that for years, and the whole time Jack was proclaiming to be a bachelor and making money off it. But I found out even more about their relationship when Kaitlin and I cleared the air." She scanned the room before continuing, "Right around the time that I left she was pregnant."

Telescope barked, and Willow assumed he was as shocked by this announcement as she was.

"She had Jack's baby? How old is the child now?" Willow realized she was much louder than Terry had been, but she couldn't help it.

"She miscarried during her second trimester. Kaitlin told me how disappointed she was."

"Poor Kaitlin," Willow said.

"That certainly wouldn't have been good for the eternal bachelor's image at the time," Terry said. "But I think it looks bad for him now too. He didn't handle the situation well, and that could still ruin his reputation."

Willow nodded. She didn't want to add any more fuel to Terry's "he did it" fire, but she had to admit that some valid points had been raised. Jack was in the area, and he had a strong motive.

Of course, Willow reminded herself, they still didn't know that Kaitlin had actually been murdered.

She heard someone at the doors to the doggie gym and turned towards it. Her father was entering the room. He was dressed in his police uniform, but that wasn't unusual. What was unusual was that he was visiting her at the gym during business hours. Maybe he was finally considering taking her up on her offer to let the police dogs train here.

Telescope ran to greet him, but he just nodded at the dog and didn't touch him.

"Hi, Dad," she said as she walked towards him. His face looked serious behind his mustache.

"I saw Terry's car outside," Frank Wells said, keeping his hands on his police belt. "When you didn't answer your door, I figured you were out here."

"And you found us," Willow said with a smile.

He didn't return it. Instead, he said, "I'm afraid I'm here to see if Ms. Gib will accompany me to the station."

"What's this about?" Terry asked.

"We have some questions related to the murder of Kaitlin Janes," Frank replied. He looked at both of their faces. "You don't seem completely shocked by this."

"We had some suspicions about the manner of her death," Willow admitted.

"I suspected foul play," Terry responded. "And I'll be happy to come with you and tell you what I know."

Frank nodded and began leading her to the door. Terry stopped and faced Willow. "Will you keep an eye on Lady Val for me?"

"Of course."

She watched Terry and her father leave the gym and shook her head. What a way to find out that this was officially a murder case!

7

Ordinarily, Willow would have loved to spend extra time training a dog to become a champion. However, between the fact that they had already had a training session that morning and her concern about the dog's owner at the police station, Willow didn't accomplish much with her that afternoon. She did play fetch with some of the pups, spent a little time with Mr. Wenderson's Great Dane, and made sure that her business was running smoothly.

When Terry arrived late that night to pick up Lady Valkyrie, she was too tired to discuss the questions she'd been asked. The next morning, Willow wondered if Terry would make her training session. She headed into the training center with Telescope to make sure it was ready if plans continued as scheduled. If they didn't, she decided that she would just let

Telescope run the entire course, show off for her, and let the dog have his day.

When everything was set, she checked her watch. She wouldn't have been surprised if Terry didn't show up, but Willow was surprised by who she saw bringing Lady Valkyrie to the gym on time that day.

"Morning," Truman Fitzpatrick said.

"Good morning," Willow said, trying not to act too confused.

Terry Gib and Truman Fitzpatrick both raised Irish setters, and their rivalry was not friendly. Even though Truman was a Pineview resident and Terry was a visitor, Willow knew that they saw each other frequently during the dog show circuit. In fact, Willow considered Truman's dog, Nero, to be their main competition.

He held onto Lady Valkyrie's leash stiffly and walked in a less fluid motion than the dog did. He had salt and pepper hair and looked on edge.

"Terry asked me to bring Lady Valkyrie in," he said by way of an explanation.

"That was nice of you."

He shrugged. "This is strange business. Terry's B&B owner dying. Now they're saying it's murder and questioning Terry."

"It is very strange," Willow agreed.

"I saw her this morning and she wasn't looking too good."

"I bet this has all been pretty stressful."

"I reckon so. I think that's why she asked me to bring her dog over. I didn't have the heart to say no. She looked so tired. Apparently, they kept her at the station real late last night."

Willow nodded. She knew that for a fact since Lady Valkyrie was picked up late into the night, but she didn't need to add any details to his account.

Truman continued. "She said that they kept her so late because there was some sort of problem with paperwork. It needed to get sorted out before she could go."

Uh oh. Willow tried to keep a neutral face as she realized some unpleasant truths. The police must think that Terry could be the murderer. She recognized her father's interrogation technique of blaming the paperwork. However, that was really an excuse to keep the suspect in the building and give them more of an opportunity to talk.

Willow didn't plan on revealing any of this to Truman. Not only was it not her business to reveal more about a police interview than Terry would be willing to share, but Truman and Nero were still their competition. She didn't want him to think that he had a leg up on them.

It sounded as if he was guessing at the serious nature of the police questions though as he continued talking. "I don't know. Whatever the reason they told her, I think if they keep you at the station that long, they probably think you're a suspect. What about you? Do you think Terry could have killed her?"

"Definitely not," Willow said, though she was portraying a confidence she didn't feel. "Terry isn't a killer."

She reached for Lady Valkyrie's leash, but Truman wasn't ready to abandon this line of conversation.

"I don't know the specifics, but I heard that she and Kaitlin had a past."

"I don't know anything about that. But I know Terry will kill me if I don't use this training session to work with her dog." She cringed the moment the words left her mouth.

"And apparently, they had a big fight a few months back. Yelling and stuff."

Lady Valkyrie was sitting patiently during this entire exchange. Telescope had begun pacing around the room.

"I hadn't heard that," Willow said. "But it sure is nice catching up with you. I haven't seen you and Nero here in a while."

Truman nodded. He had done most of his training at home, but he did like to take advantage of the gym's amenities and obstacles. Now that she thought about it, she realized that she hadn't seen Nero in at least a month - maybe two. That wasn't so strange though. With the Field Club Championship approaching, Truman probably wanted to keep his dog's abilities a secret, especially with his competition now in town.

"Yes. We've been working privately. No offense to you. What you do here is great. But I wanted to work with him one-on-one for this show."

"I understand," Willow said. She hoped if she could keep

68

him talking about dogs, he might forget the subject of interrogations. "How is Nero doing though? Does he still wag his tail in the air when he makes it over a high hurdle?"

"He – well, I guess I've taken up enough of your training time already with my blathering on," he said, finally handing the leash over to Willow. "I should let you get to work."

"That was your evil plan all along, wasn't it?" Willow teased.

"What is?"

"Taking up Lady Valkyrie's session with chit-chat so she has less time to practice?"

He chuckled. "You caught me."

Willow unhooked the dog from her leash and let her run. Telescope joined her, and the two dogs ran the perimeter of the room.

She watched them go and then turned back to Truman who was finding a place to sit.

"You don't care if I watch, do you?" he asked. "Terry didn't seem to mind."

Willow would have preferred that her archrival for the championship wasn't watching her every move, but it appeared as if she didn't have a choice unless she wanted to come off as very rude. Also, it was true that Truman had done Terry a big favor by bringing her dog here today.

"It's no problem," Willow said brightly.

She began editing the mental checklist in her head of what she should accomplish with Lady Valkyrie now that they had an observer. She didn't want to show off her special tricks, but she didn't want to focus on the obstacles that gave her little trouble either. Willow's original plan had been to work on agility trials and place cones at different distances from each other to allow Lady Valkyrie to adapt to the various amounts of space to swivel around. However, now she decided that she wanted to do something that would allow Lady Valkyrie to show off a little pizzazz.

"I've got it," she said, before calling the dogs over to her. "Let's practice the seesaw today."

This obstacle was still new to Lady Valkyrie, so it would show off her natural balance and boldness. She needed to run up a board that was diagonally pointed up, but as she moved across the board, it would swing down so she could continue right on to the ground.

Willow was very impressed with the dog's work, and Truman appeared to be too.

Terry appeared at the very end of the session and clapped as she saw Lady Valkyrie race across the seesaw. After she'd completed it, the dog raced to see her master, and the humans and Telescope followed her.

"Thank you for bringing her over here today," Terry said to Truman. "I really needed that nap. But I can take over now."

He nodded. He opened his mouth and closed it several times before finally asking, "How are you holding up?"

"I'm feeling better. Thank you."

He gave a wave to Willow and then left the gym. When she was sure that he was gone, Willow turned to Terry.

"What did you find out?"

"Firstly, Kaitlin's dog, Polly, is all right. She's staying with a young detective named Denton. He is taking care of her until they track down Kaitlin's extended family."

"That's good news," Willow agreed. "And about her death?"

"Kaitlin was definitely murdered," Terry said. "It was rat poison."

Willow raised an eyebrow. She remembered police procedure. "It seems pretty early to get those sorts of test results back already."

"They could see some of the pellet residue in the bottom of Kaitlin's coffee mugs. There were several of them in her apartment."

"So, she was poisoned multiple times?"

"Apparently in humans, the poison needs to build up in your system to become deadly. And that's what happened to Kaitlin." Terry swallowed nervously. "They said that it looked like she had been poisoned since the day that I arrived in town."

Willow placed an arm around her. The two events happening on the same day was probably more of a coincidence than anything else.

"If someone poisoned Kaitlin's coffee grounds, then the

poison could have been added before you arrived," Willow said. "It was just brewed after that."

She wanted to reassure her client. However, she also wanted answers. Willow couldn't help thinking that Terry was still keeping something from her. The police had questioned Terry for hours. There had to be another reason that they thought she was guilty.

"What sorts of questions did the police ask?"

"The sort of things that you would expect," Terry answered.

Willow waited to see if she would say anything else, but she remained quiet. Willow decided to switch gears.

"So, why did you ask Truman to bring Lady Valkyrie here?"

"Oh that," Terry said, shrugging. "I figure you should keep your friends close and your enemies closer. And the more time he spends with Lady Val, the less time he'll have to train his own dog. He probably thinks he gained some knowledge from watching her, but I'm sure you didn't show anything that could give him an advantage."

"I tried not to," Willow said.

"And besides, I was really tired this morning."

Willow led her to the side so they could sit down and finish their conversation. Maybe if Terry were more comfortable, she might be willing to open up more. The dogs laid down at their feet, ready to relax after their work with the obstacles. Willow had to admit that she felt like she was on a seesaw too. She felt like she never quite knew where the facts stood in regard to Kaitlin's death.

"I don't blame you for being tired," Willow said. "I know that my dad can be pretty persuasive and sometimes terrifying. I remember the battles of trying to borrow the car from him in high school. I imagine he's even scarier when he thinks you might have committed a crime."

"I'm afraid they might really think that I did it."

"But why?" Willow asked. "If you've told me everything, then your problems with Kaitlin during your pageant days were ancient history. And the two of you made peace recently. You did tell me everything, right?"

"Of course."

"Because," Willow said pointedly, "Truman mentioned that you and Kaitlin had a big fight a few months ago. People must have heard you yelling."

Terry hid her face in her hands. "Yes. Okay, I guess I didn't mention that. But that was only because of what happened after…"

"And what was that?"

Terry looked at her. "The fight was a few months ago. It was when I first visited Pineview right when your gym was opening. That was when I was in the market for a trainer but didn't have a competition in mind."

"I remember."

"Well, there's only one bed-and-breakfast in town that allows dogs. I didn't realize that Kaitlin owned it, and it caught me by surprise. I guess some of the emotions I've kept bottled up for years broke through."

"Unfortunately, people heard you."

"I was very angry to come across her like that. I almost didn't want to train here because I knew I'd have to live there. But then I decided I wasn't going to let her dictate my life anymore. You were the best trainer, and I wanted to work with you."

"Thanks," Willow said with a slight blush at the compliment. "But what about Kaitlin?"

"Because we were forced to be in the same town, we had to speak to one another again. That's when we cleared the air, and she told me about losing the baby. And that's when I started to feel bad about what I was going to…" She covered her mouth instead of speaking.

"Terry, if you want my help, you're going to have to level with me," Willow said, rising. "What are you hiding?"

"After the fight outside the B&B, I was approached by a businessman. He had a birthmark on his face and a really expensive watch. He said his name was Benny Gene. He wanted to buy Kaitlin's building, and she didn't want to sell. And well, since he found out about my troubles with her, he asked if I could help him sabotage her business."

"What did you tell him?" Willow asked.

"I agreed," Terry said, turning red. "But I didn't actually get a chance to do anything. And after Kaitlin and I made up, I told him that I wasn't going to help him. I was too embarrassed to tell the police this."

"And it does make you look guiltier," Willow admitted.

Terry groaned and reached for her dog.

"But," Willow continued, "you might have given us another suspect to look into too. If Benny Gene really wanted that piece of real estate, he might be willing to kill for it."

8

W illow lay in Savasana pose on her yoga mat, willing herself to relax and find her inner peace. She wanted to forget about the drama surrounding her new charge's owner for a little while. She was almost successful until she remembered that "Savasana" translated to "corpse pose," and then her mind was drawn back to Kaitlin Janes.

She didn't mind when the class ended and she was able to get to her feet again. She rolled up her mat and told Wednesday that she was going to get a drink of water. Her sister nodded but was already happily reaching for her cell phone.

Willow grabbed her reusable water bottle and headed towards the water fountain to refill it. She was glad that Wednesday had convinced her to become a member at

Namaste A While Studio. It was a friendly place and the drop-in classes offered were ideal for her busy schedule.

After hydrating, she headed back to the exercise room she had been in because Wednesday still hadn't come out. As she entered the room, she saw why. Linda, who owned the shy Yorkshire terrier, had cornered Wednesday and was giving her an earful on her opinions about Kaitlin's death.

Linda wasn't wearing her pearl necklace today, but she did have on pearl earrings and was wearing an outfit that perfectly matched her sneakers and scrunchie. Willow wasn't sure how much Zen the woman had found in class because she was sounding very catty as she spoke.

Wednesday was nodding patiently, but her eyes kept drifting down towards her cell screen.

"And you know I would never want to speak ill of the dead," said Linda.

"Of course," Wednesday agreed.

"But I do believe that she brought this upon herself. The way she lived," Linda said, shuddering. "Well, you know all about that after logging my complaints. And I do appreciate that."

"That's my job."

"Well, I think it all caught up with her. Kaitlin was a menace. She's endangered lives, and I bet she caused some deaths too. That's the sort of person she was."

Willow felt that she couldn't stay out of this conversation any longer. She walked up to the pair and smiled at them both.

"Hello, Linda. Hi, sis," she said a little too jovially. "Did I just happen to hear you talking about Kaitlin Janes?"

"I'm not one to gossip," Linda said. "I was just checking in with your sister in an official manner. As the police secretary, she handled an ongoing matter for me. Though perhaps it is finally resolved now."

"By Kaitlin's death?" Willow asked.

Linda allowed a slight shrug. "I thought she died of an illness, which would have made sense. But Wednesday here tells me that she was murdered. Somehow that seems to make even more sense."

"Wait," Willow said. "Are you saying that you have some idea who killed her?"

"Of course not. That's for the police to figure out. What I'm saying is that Kaitlin was dangerous," Linda said as a dark expression came over her face. "But, again, I'm not one to gossip. And I better get going. There's a sandwich shop that I heard had an employee who isn't wearing a hairnet. I have to see this for myself."

"And then I'm sure I'll hear all about it," Wednesday said.

Linda stared at her as if she was trying to decide if this was an insult or not. She appeared to opt to take it at face value and said her goodbyes. Willow said that she hoped she would see her and Pattie again soon.

"Wow," Willow said after Linda walked away. "Can you believe everything she said?"

"I can because I have to take down all her complaints

at the station. Half of them are nonsense, and the ones against Kaitlin were too. You've seen that bed-and-breakfast, right? You must have visited it to see a dog at some point."

Willow nodded.

"Did it look run-down and filthy to you?" Wednesday asked.

"No. Actually, it was spotless. And I know it's won awards as a dog-friendly hotel. It was praised for its attention to detail."

"Exactly," Wednesday said. "There's nothing to it. And this is Linda's schtick."

"What do you mean?"

"She always has a vendetta about something or someone. This time it had been Kaitlin. I guess next it will be that poor kid at the sandwich shop."

Willow was still focused on the possible complaint. "Well, have the police looked into the B&B yet when investigating the death?"

"They must have," Wednesday said. "But I haven't seen the report yet. I guess I haven't been keeping regular hours lately."

Willow kept her comments to herself, and the sisters headed out of the room and towards the lobby. There they ran into the studio's owner, Miranda. She was a sweet, middle-aged woman who was more flexible than Willow thought she would ever be.

She beamed at them. "How was your photo shoot before the class?"

"Honestly, it was amazing," Wednesday said. "I got all the shots I needed in about five snaps with a light filter. Hashtag – Yoga Journey. Hashtag – Finding Zen. Hashtag – Sisters Bonding."

"Hashtag – Namaste A While?" Miranda suggested.

"Hashtag – Duh!" said Wednesday.

Willow laughed.

"Of course, I'll include a shout-out to this studio," her sister said. "We love it here."

"And do you think that mentioning my studio in your online feature will attract some new customers?"

"It definitely should."

"Well, then why don't you two enjoy a smoothie at the juice bar? My treat in exchange for the advertising."

They thanked her and headed over to the bar. Wednesday was practically skipping.

"I should have thought about this before," she said. "Besides being delicious, the smoothies will look great in my pictures. Choose a flavor with bright colors."

Willow indulged her and told the man behind the juice bar that she would have the "brightest" smoothie they had. Wednesday chose a pineapple flavor, saying the yellow would look nice next to her hair.

Willow smiled at her sister. "This 'Week in My Life' project seems to be going really well."

"I feel like I'm killing it," she agreed, beaming back at her.

Their smoothies were handed back to them, and Willow was impressed to see that hers was almost neon blue. She wasn't sure what was in it, but she was willing to try it.

"Smile," Wednesday said.

Willow obeyed the instructions, trying to keep her drink's straw out of her face. Wednesday kept snapping pics and changing filters. Willow was dimly aware of movement behind her but couldn't see what was happening because of the flash from the photos.

When they were finished, Wednesday assured her that they had gotten some great shots. Willow looked behind her to see what was moving and noticed Miranda was looking a little embarrassed. She held a painting of a scenic beach behind her back, but it was too large to be hidden.

She smiled reassuringly at the woman as she realized what had happened. Miranda had been changing the calming artwork on the walls to flyers and signs that displayed the studio's name and logo so they would be captured in the photos. That wasn't a bad trick. Maybe she should consider doing that when Wednesday visited the doggie gym.

Willow tried her blue smoothie. She still couldn't identify all the flavors, but she found it tasty. Wednesday was scrolling through the pictures as Willow asked, "Are you sure there's nothing to Linda's complaints?"

"I don't think so," Wednesday said. "She liked to complain about everything."

"But this time the person she complained about was poisoned."

"Let's not talk about poison while we're drinking."

"I'll talk suspects instead," said Willow conspiratorially. "They're adding up. The police seem to suspect Terry, but I think there are other options. Linda was unhappy with Kaitlin. Benny Gene wanted to buy her building and she refused. And Jack Grim was her ex-boyfriend who didn't want her to reveal secrets about their relationship. Benny might not have been in town, but the others definitely were."

"Are you officially investigating?" Wednesday asked, sipping her smoothie.

"I just don't like seeing Terry accused of a crime when there are other possibilities."

Wednesday pouted. "You know that I'd love to help with another round of sleuthing. But I do have an awful lot on my plate right now. I have a lot of paperwork at the station this week, and I have to write Dad's bio which I haven't even started yet, not to mention that I have to keep this week in my life exciting. Oh, but that last part will be easy. You know what it's time for now?"

Willow frowned as she listened to what her sister had on her plate. "You haven't been avoiding doing Dad's bio, have you?"

"You're not avoiding setting up your Tinder account, are you?" Wednesday retorted.

"Not exactly."

"Then, let's get started!"

Wednesday excitedly explained how she would record short videos or "Instastories" of Willow setting up her Tinder account and if she got matched with anyone. They would be on SnapChat, Instagram, and a part of Wednesday's "Week." There would be subtle differences in what they filmed for the different platforms, and Willow just hoped that in one of these short videos she looked cool, or at least sympathetic.

"Stand by that wall," Wednesday instructed. "The barn wood texture will make your outfit pop, and it can be a picture we add to your profile."

Willow agreed with her sister's eye about the outfit and hoped that she was right about using Tinder too. After the picture was taken, she realized that one of Miranda's logos for Namaste A While was in the background. Great. Now everyone would know where all the embarrassment in her life was taking place.

Wednesday began filming videos of them setting up her profile.

"This might be embarrassing to have filmed," Willow began. The filming didn't stop, so she continued. "But, tell me a little more about what I'm signing up for. I've heard about Tinder, of course. But I guess I didn't always pay attention. It wasn't something I thought I'd ever use."

"It's very easy," Wednesday explained. "The app knows your location."

"Creepy."

"Useful. And it shows you potential dates in the area. It suggests matches based on common interests. You can see pictures and profiles to determine if you think you'd get along. If you like the person, you swipe right, and if you don't like him, you swipe left. If you both swipe right, then you get to chat with one another. Simple, right?"

"I don't know," Willow said, starting to get cold feet. "This sounds like a hookup app."

"Maybe some people use it that way, but there are also a ton of people who found the person they married on Tinder."

"And if I'm looking for something in between those two options?"

"Come on, Wills. Swipe right for this and finish setting up your profile."

"Fine."

She figured it would probably look worse if she backed out of it now since this was all being recorded. Besides, she didn't have to meet with anyone that she didn't think she might actually like, and there was also the possibility that she would be matched with someone really great. She wanted to get back in the dating game, and this was apparently how people did it nowadays.

She finished her profile and took a deep breath.

"Great job," Wednesday said. "Now you get to see your matches."

"This is the part that scares me," Willow admitted. "What if all the people I'm matched with I don't find attractive?

What if they all remind me of Benjamin? What if I'm acciden-
tally paired with someone who doesn't like dogs?"

"It's going to be all right. You don't have to meet anyone
you don't think you'll like. And a bad date isn't the end of
the world."

"It feels like it right now."

Wednesday grabbed her phone. "Look, here's your first
match. Benny. He's a businessman and a fellow yoga devotee.
The app says he's used this studio before."

"That doesn't sound too bad," Willow said, turning the
screen so she could see it. The man had slicked back hair and
a professional suit on in his picture. There was something
else about him. "Does that look like a birthmark on
his face?"

"He's still pretty cute," Wednesday said. "But if you don't
like him, we can swipe left."

"No!" Willow said, grabbing the phone.

"You don't have to like the first person you're paired
with," Wednesday said, practically cowering from the
outburst.

"It's not that," Willow said. "I think that this Benny is
Benny Gene."

"One of your potential suspects?"

Willow nodded. "You said that this app is based on
location?"

"Right."

"So, we'd only be paired if he was in the area?" Willow

said. "That's very interesting. Because then it seems like he might have been in Pineview to poison Kaitlin after all."

"What are you going to do?"

"I'll accept the match and see if we can go on a date. Then I could interview him and see what he really knows about Kaitlin's death."

"So, you're using your dating app to try and interrogate a murder suspect?"

"I guess that's one way of looking at it," Willow said.

"This might be why you're still single," Wednesday teased.

Willow ignored her and swiped right.

9

"*Concerns About Dating* is taking the lead, but now it's *Business Woes*," Willow said to herself as she were announcing horses racing instead of the thoughts running around her head. She gave her kitchen counter a hearty scrub as she concluded. "And finally, it's *Who Really Killed Kaitlin?* They're turning the corner. It's a photo finish!"

"Who's racing?" Griffin asked.

Willow dropped her sponge in embarrassment. She hadn't realized anyone was in the room, but Griffin had walked in carrying a box of donuts, and Telescope was standing next to him.

"Traitor," Willow whispered to the dog. He just wagged his tail, not seeming at all concerned that he hadn't alerted her to another person's presence and let her embarrass herself.

"So, what's going on?"

"I was just giving the commentary on which thoughts were in my head."

Griffin held back laughter in his smile. "I'd say that's funny, but you only clean like this when you're stressed."

"I clean," Willow said defensively.

"Yes," he said. "But not with so much scrubbing vigor. What's wrong?"

"Nothing and everything."

"Would a donut help?" he asked, opening the box to showcase the colorful treats he'd selected. "I thought they might go well with our coffee today."

"Sounds perfect. Just let me wash up so I don't have a Clorox-Flavored Donut."

She took off her gloves and washed her hands while Griffin poured them their morning cups of joe. She accepted her mug and selected a Boston cream.

"So, what's bothering you today? It sounded like there were a few contenders."

"Well, first I was worried about my business."

"About that doggie spa?" Griffin asked.

"If Lady Valkyrie doesn't win, I won't be able to afford the renovations for it. And I know you'd need to start it soon so it would still fall under your current contract."

"Let's not talk about contracts," he said, focusing on his coffee instead.

"And I've also started worrying about online reviews.

After all this *week in Wednesday's life* stuff, I've realized how important they are. So, I made sure that my doggie gym was on Yelp, but now I'm freaking out about potential reviews. What if Linda decides to make a complaint?"

"What could she complain about?" Griffin asked, sounding reasonable. "I've never seen an unhappy dog at your gym."

"Thanks," Willow said, smiling. He had a way of making her feel better. "Plus, I guess I shouldn't worry about Linda too much. She might even end up in prison for murder."

"Murder?" he asked, almost spitting his coffee out.

"I guess I am jumping a bit too far ahead," Willow admitted. "But she is on my list of suspects."

Griffin set his coffee down. "Why do you think she could be a killer?"

"She made a lot of complaints against Kaitlin Janes," Willow said. "And the way she was talking about her at the yoga studio made it sound like she was not at all sorry that Kaitlin was dead."

"Could she have done it?"

"If she was making complaints about the B&B, then she needed to have been inside it at some time before. Maybe she could have poisoned Kaitlin's coffee grounds on that visit."

"And then Kaitlin was poisoning herself every time she brewed herself a cup of coffee," Griffin said.

Willow set her coffee mug on the counter and stared at it.

"What a mean way to kill someone."

"Agreed," said Griffin. "Not that there's ever really a nice way to murder someone. But I love my morning coffee, especially when it's with someone you like to talk to. It would be cruel to kill someone that way."

"And yet, someone did," Willow said. "And I want to figure out who."

"We made a pretty good team the last time we investigated a case together," Griffin said, leaning on the island counter and getting closer to her.

"I had to drag you kicking and screaming to help me," Willow teased.

"That was a complicated situation. There were things I couldn't tell you," he said in protest.

"Yeah, yeah," she said, pretending to push him away.

"But now I tell you everything."

Willow wasn't quite sure how to respond to that. She picked her coffee mug up again, sniffed it and declared it poison-free. She took a big swig.

"Who else do you have as a suspect?" Griffin asked, retreating back to his own cup.

"Jack Grim. He was Kaitlin's bachelor ex-boyfriend."
"Huh?"

She recapped Jack and Kaitlin's history, but then added, "If they were an on-again, off-again relationship back then, it's possible they still were up until her death. I bet she would have let him into her apartment if he asked to come in. And that could have given him an opportunity to add the poison to her coffee grounds."

"Anyone else?"

"For right now, I'm trying to believe that it wasn't Terry," she said with a sigh. "And I should know more about Benny as a suspect later tonight. That's everyone right now."

"Let me know if you need the help of a handsome contractor at all on this case."

She chuckled. "I will. Even though I know you're not paid enough to go on all these dangerous adventures with me. Stakeouts and questioning."

"I like going on adventures with you," he said simply.

Willow looked down at the donut box. She picked up a strawberry sprinkle one and took a bite.

"Anything else bothering you?" he asked as he selected another donut too.

"Well, the third thing was about dating," Willow said, playing with her food.

"Really?"

"Because the other areas of my life have started to get on track, I was thinking I should start dating again. You know, it's the final thing I have to do to feel like I've really kicked my ex to the curb."

Griffin nodded. "I get that. You've made a new home for yourself. You've started a successful business and are training another champion dog."

"Even if there have been some bumps along that road."

"You've done great for yourself, and if dating is the final step you feel you need to take, then I say go for it."

"You think so?" she asked. "I'd been feeling confident about it until it was actually time to do it. It's like I climbed up to the top of the diving board, but now I don't want to jump."

"That's a perfect metaphor because I was going to say that you'll need to take a leap of faith. So, leap off of that diving board."

"Into the deep end?"

"Exactly."

They both laughed. Telescope joined in with a hearty bark.

"Hey," Griffin said suddenly. "Remember the pool that they had at the high school?"

"I've tried to forget it," Willow said. "And let's not start reminiscing about our time in school. Wednesday has been reminding me about the terrible dates I went on then."

Griffin looked thoughtful. "Maybe you should have dated someone else."

"Maybe," Willow said, not committing to anything. "But I'm trying not to dwell on the past. I'm all about moving forward."

Griffin sat on a kitchen stool next to her. "Are you looking for ideas on what to do for a date?"

"I guess I could accept suggestions."

"I have a few thoughts on the matter," he said. "I'm a big fan of picnics. But there's also an Italian restaurant that opened up after you first moved away. For a casual dining experience, there's a bar called Frankie's that has live music every Friday night. I also know a few places where you have an uninterrupted view of the night sky."

"I bet you're a better dating coach than Jack," Willow said. "Those all sound like a lot of fun."

"Of course, on a date, it really just matters who you're with."

He was staring at her and Willow needed to get away from that gaze. She brought her mug over to the sink and began to rinse it. He followed her and picked up the dish towel to dry.

They fell into an easy pattern with the two dishes.

When the water was off, Willow said, "I should tell Terry about those dating ideas that you suggested. She was trying to get into the dating game too. Of course, things haven't been going her way recently."

"Yeah," Griffin scoffed. "I remember being the prime suspect in a murder case. It's not fun."

"Then again, she's had bad luck in relation to Kaitlin before too. Apparently, they had problems when they did beauty pageants together. Kaitlin was Terry's coach, and they had a falling out."

"Wait a minute," Griffin said, taking a step back. "What's Terry's full name again?"

"Gib."

"Could she have shortened her name?" Griffin asked. "Could she have been a Teresa Gib?"

Willow nodded. "I think so."

"I can't believe I didn't make the connection before," Griffin said. He covered his face with his hand.

"What connection?"

"Um, when Terry spoke about her pageants, did she ever mention the Miss World competition?"

"Not specifically. She did mention the semifinals for something though. Why?"

Griffin was turning red. "Because I've seen her performance. I think it's still making the rounds on the internet."

"What happened?"

"A wardrobe malfunction. A major one."

"Oh no," Willow said, covering her mouth. "Poor Terry."

"It must have been really embarrassing. It took her a moment to realize that anything was wrong with her dress. And then she went berserk."

"And you watched this?"

"About a dozen times." He cleared his throat when he saw the glare that Willow was giving him. "When I was in high school. It was just when I was in high school."

"I'm glad we're not reminiscing about those days," Willow said. "I can't imagine wanting to watch someone embarrass themselves like that, especially more than once."

Griffin looked abashed. "I want to do what I can to help her and you."

"Well, I'll keep that under consideration," she said. "But I think I should let you get to work. I have things I need to do too."

She closed the box of donuts and began to leave the kitchen.

"Wait, Wills. Don't be mad at me."

"I'm not mad," she said, and she wasn't – not exactly. "But I do have things that I need to do. I have to talk to Terry about this, and then I need to get ready for my date tonight."

"Wait," he said, looking shocked. "You already have a date set up?"

"That's right. With a businessman."

"Well, I hope you have a really great time," he said, not sounding like he meant it at all.

"Thank you. I bet I will," she said defensively.

She felt no need to tell him that the main reason she was going out was to interview a suspect. No, there was no reason to do that at all.

10

W illow had called Terry immediately after speaking to Griffin, and Terry agreed that they should meet to talk about the pageant sabotage in person. She had been planning to take Lady Valkyrie for a walk in the park anyway and suggested they meet there in twenty minutes.

It would only take half that time to ready Telescope and drive there, so Willow offered to take Wednesday's cat, Rover, for a walk as well. She felt she owed her sister something for her help picking out outfits, both for her meeting with the dating guru/suspect and for going on a date/talking to a suspect.

She called Wednesday and made the offer. Her sister gratefully accepted, but also warned, "Rover has been pretty grumpy lately. She's almost all recovered, but the stitches in her tail have been messing with her mojo."

Rover had injured herself drinking out of the toilet. She had been so enthusiastic that she had bumped some of Wednesday's decorations off of the top shelf of the toilet, including a potted plant. The ceramic had broken, and Rover had been so frightened by the noise that she fell while scampering away. Luckily, she had survived with only a cut on her tail, but Wednesday said it inspired her to make sure that her bathroom door always remained closed.

"Maybe this will help her feel more like herself," Willow suggested. "She loves going on walks."

They agreed, and Willow promised to be there shortly. She put Telescope in his harness, and they headed out to pick up his "cousin."

Willow drove to Wednesday's house and used her spare key to unlock the door. Rover was waiting at the door. The cat stared up at them expectantly.

"Want to go for a walk?" Willow asked.

Rover wagged her tail, but that seemed to hurt her because then she mewed.

"Don't worry," Willow said. "We know you're excited to see us."

She put a leash on Rover and put the two animals in her car. Telescope didn't always have patience with the cat who thought she was a dog, but he seemed to understand that she was feeling poorly. He sat close to her on the ride to show his support.

Willow started leading them around the park. There was a path that led around the outskirts of a pine forest and allowed Willow to keep an eye out for Terry's arrival.

She hoped that she wouldn't run into anyone else that she would have to make small talk with. Luckily, the only people she saw at the park were a young couple that were too interested in each other to notice her, and Mr. Wenderson who was using the techniques he had learned from Willow to convince his large dog to heel.

Rover seemed to enjoy the walk. Willow noticed that the cat only seemed distracted when she tried to wag her tail, but Telescope kept pace with Rover, making sure she didn't feel alone.

When Willow saw Terry and Lady Valkyrie, she led the walk right towards them.

"Thanks for meeting me here," Terry said. "I think the animals will like the fresh air."

"I think they will," Willow agreed. "But I wish this meeting wasn't necessary. It seems like you keep hiding things from me."

"I'm sorry," Terry said. "I'm used to trying to forget that Miss World ever happened."

She started leading Lady Valkyrie down the path, Willow sensed it was so her client wouldn't have to look at her.

However, Willow quickly caught up with her two animals in tow.

"I could understand that under normal circumstances," Willow said. "But this is a murder case now. If you keep something a secret, when it eventually comes out into the open, it makes you look even more suspicious."

"You don't have to tell me about things coming out in the open," Terry said with a scoff. "I experienced that firsthand during the semifinals."

"That's what caused you to quit pageants and leave Kaitlin?"

"Why do you need to know all this?" Terry asked.

"You were the one who asked me to look into her death, remember? You said she was murdered and I should track down Jack. Now it's clear that she was killed, and I think the police are looking at the wrong woman. I want to help. But if you don't want me to, I won't."

Willow tugged on Tele and Rover's leashes indicating they should stop. Terry took a few more steps and then turned.

"No. I do want your help. And I appreciate everything you've done. I just don't like talking about this."

"I'm sorry, but I need to know everything."

Terry took a deep breath and held onto the dog leash tighter than was necessary and started talking. "The full story is that Kaitlin and I were apparently offered money to throw the Miss World competition. But I didn't know about it at the time. Maybe Kaitlin knew I wouldn't have wanted to. I'd worked so hard to get there. But she made sure that I lost anyway."

"In a drastic way."

Terry continued to avoid eye contact. "Did you watch the clip of it?"

"No."

"You're probably the only one who hasn't," she said, finally looking at her. "I changed my hair color and started going by Terry to try and avoid being recognized. Everyone had already seen so much of me."

"I heard it was a wardrobe malfunction?"

"Brought on by Kaitlin." Terry nodded. "It happened during my question-and-answer portion of the competition. The snip she made on the spaghetti strap on my evening dress put me all over Google images. It was the most embarrassing moment of my life."

"And it looks like a motive for murder," Willow said.

"I was furious about it for a long time," Terry agreed. "Especially when I learned about the money she got for that stunt. I didn't get a penny of it. She ruined my life, and she kept all the cash."

"Why didn't you tell anyone about her sabotage before?"

"I figured no one would believe me if I said I didn't know about her plan. They would all wonder how I couldn't have known."

Willow nodded supportively.

"I decided just to get away from it all and find a new place in the world."

The pair continued on their walk with the animals keeping easy pace together despite their different sizes. Willow briefly registered that Lady Valkyrie wasn't distracted by a cat in their midst and hoped this would be a good indication of her focus in the ring. Then, she turned back to Terry's story.

"And you found it with your dogs, but they ended up bringing you into contact with her again."

"That's right. And my surprise at seeing her led to our argument outside the bed-and-breakfast and that businessman asking me to help sabotage her," Terry said. "But we made peace before she died. I understood where she was coming from, and I was starting to forgive her for what she did during the pageant."

"Wait. Where was she coming from at that time? It still sounds malicious to me."

"I don't condone the choice she made. I definitely think she should have told me about the bribe. And she could have let me decide a less embarrassing way to throw the competition if I was going to," Terry said. "But she had just found out she was pregnant. And she wasn't sure how helpful Jack would be. She needed the money to take care of her child."

"By betraying her friend," Willow said. She wasn't quite ready to forgive Kaitlin's behavior. She couldn't imagine how mortifying it would feel if she'd been in the same circumstance – especially since the event was televised.

"I know," Terry said quietly. "But she lost the baby. I felt like she already paid a penance, and she was trying to be a better person."

They were silent for a few minutes. Then Willow added, "And regardless of what she did, she shouldn't have been murdered."

"I didn't tell the police about this because I was afraid it would make me look guilty and they already think I did it," Terry said. "I didn't tell them what I told you about Benny Gene either."

"About him asking you to sabotage her B&B?"

"I thought that put me in a poor light too. But I've been thinking about it lately, and I should tell them. What if his actions played a role in her death?"

"He did want the property," Willow said. "And if she wasn't agreeing to sell, and he had lost his assistant in sabotage, maybe he upped the ante. Maybe he progressed to murder."

Terry was thoughtful. "I didn't consider him a suspect at first because I thought that having someone die at the B&B would decrease its value. Who would want the ghost of a murder hanging over a property?"

"I hadn't considered that," Willow said. "And you do have a point. But maybe he wasn't worried about that. Maybe he thought that the bed-and-breakfast's stellar reputation and his business flare could outweigh the stigma and erase the superstitions."

"Maybe," Terry said, biting her lip. "But, no. He couldn't have done it."

"Why not?"

"He doesn't live here. When he offered me the opportunity to sabotage her, he told me he would be leaving town right away. He wasn't here when she was murdered."

"I'm afraid that's not correct," Willow said.

"What do you mean?"

"Benny is in town, and I've got a date with him tonight."

11

That night, outside of the restaurant, Willow had butterflies in her stomach. She couldn't tell whether this was because she finally realized that she had agreed to dinner with a potential poisoner or if it was because this was her first date since her divorce. Even if there was an ulterior motive for the meeting, it didn't invalidate that she was at a fancy establishment about to enjoy a meal with a man she had "been matched with."

She caught her reflection in the restaurant's glass window and decided she looked all right. She was wearing a gray dress that was suitable for any occasion. It was fitting because she didn't know this restaurant at all. She had let Benny chose the location, and he chose a place in the next town over.

She had spiced up the dress with a few colorful jewelry

pieces that Wednesday had suggested, and she thought that her hair looked nice down instead of pulled back in her usual ponytail.

She took a deep breath and entered through the glass door. She was impressed. The lobby was fancy without being overdone, and the smells wafting into the room were intoxicating.

The hostess asked if she would like a table and Willow froze. What were you supposed to say on a first date? She had met her ex-husband in college, and most of their first meals together had been in the dining hall. Should she get a table and have Benny meet her there? Should she look around and see if he had done the same thing? Should she sit at the bar? Maybe she should just go home.

In the end, she told the hostess that she was waiting for someone and stood awkwardly to the side. It felt like she had been waiting forever and started to consider whether she had been stood up, but then she rationalized that probably only five minutes had actually passed.

It gave her enough time to collect her thoughts about Benny. While his profile made him seem likable by including his love of yoga and that he liked to travel, she had other information that she could use to draw an opinion of him. If he was willing to resort to sabotage or blackmail to gain a property, he was probably a shark of a businessman. There was also the likelihood that he could be a cold-blooded killer.

However, the man who greeted her after walking through the door didn't act like a killer.

"Willow," he said, moving closer to her. "You look even lovelier in person."

"Thank you. You look lovely – I mean, good, too."

She kicked herself internally, but he smiled and placed a hand on the small of her back to lead her to a table. They sat at a booth that had a clear view of the bar and the rest of the restaurant. There were candles on their table and Willow thought it was romantic.

"This is supposed to be an up-and-coming restaurant. I've heard good things about it."

"Everything on the menu looks good," Willow said, as she opened it and perused the courses.

"I like to sample different restaurants and see if they could be a worthwhile investment to add to one of our hotels. Or if there are any chefs worth stealing away."

"I see," Willow said. "This is a work date as well. You're mixing business and pleasure."

"It's hard for me to turn off," he admitted. "But the main reason I chose this place was because I heard the menu was varied. It can be difficult to choose a place for a first date, but I was sure there was something you would like here."

"There is something here I like," Willow said, proud of herself for sounding so flirty.

He smiled at her. "I'm glad we were matched."

"Me too," Willow said. "But I was a little surprised that we were?"

"Because of the differences in our businesses?" he asked.

"Because I live in Pineview," she said, trying to work the questions she had for him into their conversation naturally. "I was surprised that they matched me with someone the next town over."

"I used to stay in Pineview, but I moved here because it was closer to my current business project."

"Oh? Where did you stay in Pineview?" Willow asked. "I know most of the places in the area. Sometimes people are traveling with a dog to come and train with me, and they ask where the best place to stay is."

"Do people travel far to train with you?" he asked.

In case he was changing the conversation to show interest in her and wasn't trying to avoid answering her question, she decided to answer.

"Sometimes," she said. "At my last location, I had people coming from two states away to train with me. I'm just starting to gain a reputation again here, but I do have one woman from out of town traveling to work with me and prepare for a championship. And, of course, I work with locals too. I like the variety of working with show dogs and pets."

"Fascinating," he said, and she thought he really meant it.

"Are you a dog person?"

"If I say no will you get up and walk away right now?" he joked.

"Definitely," she said, pretending to rise from her seat already.

"I do love dogs. Who doesn't?" he said. "But I'm not in a

situation to have one of my own right now. I travel too much, and I would hate to leave him alone."

"There are many hotels that cater to people with pets."

"But my job wouldn't. I don't think I could bring him into a meeting with me," he said with a little sigh. "I bet you have a dog of your own, don't you?"

"Of course. His name is Telescope, but I call him Tele."

"Do you have a million stories about him that you want to tell me and you're refraining because you don't want to seem like a crazy dog lady on our first date?"

"Maybe."

He chuckled. "Go right ahead and tell me. I'd love to hear all about him."

"You're sure? You're opening a can of worms here," Willow said.

"Go on," he assured her. "Then, I can live vicariously through a dog owner."

"I'll give you the highlights. I rescued Tele and that was probably the best thing I've ever done. He's about this big," she said, indicating his size. "He's a chihuahua mix of some kind. And he only has three legs, but he doesn't let that slow him down at all."

"He sounds like an amazing dog."

"He really is."

"I had a remarkable dog growing up," Benny said. "That is if you don't mind me gushing about my childhood dog for a moment."

"Not at all."

"His name was Roscoe, and he was such a brave guy. He saved my life once. When I was a little boy, I went running into the street after a ball. A car was coming, and I didn't see it. But Roscoe did. He pushed me to safety, but he got clipped by the car in the process."

Willow gasped, but then told herself to remain cool. After all, this had happened a long time ago.

"He didn't die. Don't worry. But he lost the use of his back legs. We got a wheelchair for him, and he would still do his best to protect me. He lived to be fifteen years old. My Roscoe," he said. "But look at me getting emotional. I might have to walk to my hotel down the street and get a new shirt if I get too many teardrops on it."

Willow handed him a napkin. "It's all right. And you know what? Tele saved my life too."

"Oh?"

"That's right. There was a dangerous man in my backyard, and he tripped him so he couldn't hurt me."

"He sounds like a very impressive dog too. We're both lucky to have had pets like that." He leaned across the table. "So, what are you thinking now?"

"About dinner?" Willow asked. "I was thinking about trying the New York strip steak here. The sides look good for it too. What about you?"

He retreated back to his menu. "Probably the chicken parm. It's pretty hard to mess that up."

Willow laughed. The waiter came by their table, and she was disappointed by the interruption. She was actually having a good time. They placed their orders, and Benny selected a bottle of wine for the occasion.

Willow realized that despite how well the first date aspect of this happened to be, she needed to get some answers about his possible involvement in the murder too.

"So, you didn't answer my question before."

"Pardon?"

"About where you stayed in Pineview."

"Oh. It was a B&B on Main Street. Cute little place. You'd like it. They allow dogs there."

"I know it," Willow said. "Of course, there's been a bit of a tragedy there now."

"What sort of tragedy?"

"The owner died recently. Everyone in town was talking about it."

"Really? That's interesting and sad. I actually met the woman."

"You did?"

He nodded. "I was thinking of buying the property, but she refused to sell."

"Maybe there might be a silver lining in all this then?" Willow suggested. "Maybe you'll be able to get the property after all?"

"Maybe," Benny agreed. "But I've moved onto some other projects now. I'll have to see if it's worth revisiting. And, of course, a death at a location can decrease the value of it. It stops some guests from wanting to travel there."

"Maybe you can get an even better price for it now?" Willow said.

"I don't know."

The waiter returned with their bottle and poured them both a glass. Though not a connoisseur, Willow thought that she made the appropriate comments about the taste.

"Are you a big fan of wine?" Benny asked.

"I'm a bigger fan of coffee," she joked. "But I like any good drink."

"While I was surveying the local area, I found an excellent place if you're into craft beer."

"I am."

"They have over a hundred types on tap, and it's actually called Tapped."

Though Willow was interested in the place, there was other information she wanted more.

"That does sound like a great place. Is it close to here?" she asked with a giggle to seem as if she were just teasing him instead of interrogating. "Is that really why you moved out of the B&B? Because it sounded like you were already settled there?"

"Well," Benny said, "Tapped is a little further away. But the property I'm staying at now has hired me for a consulting job, and I wanted the experience of staying there. It helps me to understand the client more if I'm in the center of the action.

And it really is just down the street from here. It's a beautiful place."

"Do you do a lot of work for hotels?" Willow asked.

"I'd say that's where the bulk of my investments and consulting jobs are located."

Willow touched the top of her wine glass with her fingers, hoping she was making her questions sound flirty and not inquisitorial.

"If you're more of a hotel guy, why were you interested in the B&B?"

"Well, I've been wanting to expand my portfolio in the area, and I thought it was a nice place. It had won awards and was well-received, but it seems as if the owner wasn't very organized. I thought she might even appreciate my offer to buy her out. But I was wrong. She turned me down point blank."

"I bet you're a guy who is not turned down very often."

"I'd like to think that's true," he said with a smile.

Willow took another sip of wine. "You know, I thought maybe the app was malfunctioning. Because of all the location-based stuff. But it said that you've been to Namaste A While studio. Is that right?"

"It is. I'm a big fan of yoga."

"I haven't seen you there," she said, making a pouty face to show her disappointment at the thought.

"Recently I've been taking morning runs before work. My current hotel has something novel called a running concierge.

He leads a group of runners through different parts of the surrounding area."

"Do you ever run in Pineview?"

"Sure. And Main Street is absolutely beautiful in the morning, and everyone is friendly and happy to be out in the fresh air."

"Main Street? So, you'd run right by the B&B?"

"I guess so," he said. "But there are a lot of lovely sights on that road. Your hometown is very picturesque. And you sure like talking about it a lot."

"Do I?" Willow asked. She had been, but that was because she was questioning him in relation to a crime.

"I don't mind," he said quickly.

"I guess I'm proud to call it my home again," Willow said, trying to come up with an explanation that was partly true. "I grew up here, and I do have roots here. But I was away for a while. For college. And I lived in Chicago as well."

"Ah, the Windy City. I've been there before. Great theater. Great pizza. Great Lakes!"

Willow laughed, and then said, "I liked it a lot. But there were some things I needed to get away from. And this feels like home now."

"Always good to have a home. But I'm afraid I'm traveling most of the time. New York City is my base."

"They have great pizza too," she joked.

"The best," he challenged.

"Too close to call," Willow said. "They're different."

She felt his eyes on her, and she looked away, feeling excited but shy.

"So," he said, and she had to turn back to look at his face. "Where does the name Willow come from? Are you named after the tree for a reason?"

"It's a family name. I told you I had roots here."

He groaned good-naturedly.

"Willow was my aunt's last name. She was one of my favorite people. She passed away last year, but she made sure I inherited her house and land to buy my dog gym. My recent success is all due to her."

Their meals arrived, and they both declared their dishes to be perfect. Willow was having a wonderful time. The conversation flowed easily. They talked more about yoga and their favorite poses. They bonded on their shared love of Zen and "finding their best life."

By the time they finished dessert, Willow was smitten. Her date wasn't the shark of the business world that she worried he might be. It also didn't seem like he could be the killer if he were so blasé about acquiring the bed-and-breakfast now.

She left the restaurant with a pep in her step and a kiss on her cheek. She couldn't help but smile. She had cleared a suspected, and she had successfully re-entered the dating world.

Benny would be a perfect person to start dating too because he lived outside of her town and that would guarantee that they would begin casually. She wasn't ready for an extreme commitment at the moment. That was too intimidating. She just wanted a nice man that she would like to spend time with. Benny seemed to fit the bill.

She headed towards her car but allowed a final look back at the restaurant that had been the location of a perfect first date. She saw something but squinted to make sure that she was seeing this right.

It was Griffin. He was entering the restaurant alone. Despite her contented feelings a moment ago, Willow felt herself frowning.

What was Griffin doing there? This was a semi-fancy restaurant and the perfect place for a date. Was he meeting someone there? Who was it? Griffin had never mentioned a date over their morning cups of coffee.

But why should he? He was her contractor. Yes, they were friendly, and being pushed into investigating a case had only made them seem closer. However, that didn't mean that he needed to tell her all his plans.

She wanted to keep her business and personal life separate, and she was going to. Griffin was business, and Benny was personal. At least, as long as he remained off her suspect list, he could be personal.

But the question kept nagging her: why was Griffin here?

12

The next morning, Willow stirred her coffee angrily at her kitchen counter. Today was a day Willow's hatred of mornings was thriving. Not only did she have to force herself out of bed and face the day when she'd much rather be under the covers cuddling with Tele, but it also seemed that everything she had heard since she had gotten up was bad news.

Terry had to cancel their morning training session. She'd been called in for questioning at the police station again. After their talk and walk with the animals, Terry had been debating telling the police about Benny's scheme to sabotage Kaitlin. She had finally decided to do it, but the plan seemed to have backfired. They had hauled her back in for questioning instead of finding Benny.

Willow also didn't like being reminded of Benny's scheme. He had seemed like the perfect gentleman at dinner, but he was the same man who had asked a woman he barely knew to destroy someone's business for his personal gain.

Willow's phone buzzed. She didn't feel like looking at it because she figured it would be more bad news. Curiosity eventually won out. After all, there might have been a new development about the murder.

It was a message from Wednesday asking why Willow ignored her texts from last night.

Willow didn't want to admit that she had been annoyed by seeing Griffin show up at the restaurant and was trying to keep the memory of her wonderful first date alive before she shared it with anyone. She typed in that she was sorry, but before she could reply more, Wednesday called her.

"I promise I was planning on calling you today anyway," Willow said.

"Don't be mad," Wednesday said, at almost the same time.

Willow groaned. "That's never a good way to begin a conversation."

"I didn't have anything exciting to add to my pics last night, so I headed to the restaurant you went to hoping to bump into you after your date."

"Annoyed, but not mad," Willow said.

"Anyway, you had left already. But I saw Benny with someone else."

"Another woman?" Willow asked. Why did she feel her

heart sinking like that? It had just been one date. Sure, it had seemed like the perfect date at the time, but they hadn't made any promises to one another.

She braced herself to hear the description of what the other woman looked like but was not prepared for what Wednesday actually said.

"No. With Griffin!"

"What? No. I don't believe it," Willow said. "No way."

"I'm texting you the photo evidence right now. Griffin and Benny met up last night."

Willow set her phone to speaker mode and placed it on the counter. She waited for the picture to upload, figuring that this was somehow Wednesday's version of a practical joke. They had been at the same restaurant, but they weren't meeting each other. Why would Griffin want to see Benny? Or vice versa?

However, as the picture appeared and Willow saw it, she realized that this was not a joke.

"Are you still there?" Wednesday asked.

"Yeah," Willow said, remembering that she was still on the phone.

"Can you see the picture?"

"You were right," she admitted, picking up the phone for closer inspection. "It looks like Benny and Griffin did meet."

In the picture, they were sitting at the bar near the restaurant's large window. Griffin was nursing a beer and looking somewhat serious. Benny had switched from wine to something on the rocks and seemed to be laughing. What could they be talking about?

"Isn't this juicy? How should I best spin it for the 'Week in My Life'?"

"What?" Willow said, nearly dropping her phone. "There is no spin."

"The two men in your life are meeting, and you don't think it's an exciting development?" Wednesday asked incredulously.

Willow bit her tongue. Even if she thought that was true, she wouldn't want this broadcast all over the internet for everyone to see. It wasn't even a part of *her* week in the life – it was her sister's. She would seem like the butt of a joke in a situation that didn't seem very funny to her at all.

"Wends, there's no story here," Willow said, sounding as convincing as she could. "They are not *two men in my life,* and they're just having a drink."

"There were empty seats at the bar. It looks like they wanted to talk about something. What do you think it was?"

"Probably sports."

"What if they were talking about you?"

"Why would they be talking about me?" she said dismissively. Though, truthfully, part of her did want to hear what her sister's answer would be.

"Well, you did say it was a good date, right?"

"Yes," Willow admitted with a sigh. "It seemed like the perfect first date. Benny isn't a killer. He's charming and smart. He loves dogs. And if Griffin hasn't scared him off, I'd love to see him again."

"You think Griffin could have scared him off?" Wednesday asked in gossip-mode again.

Willow could have hit herself in the forehead. "That's not what I meant."

"Because it does seem like there are some sparks between you two. I know you don't want to admit that, but—"

"There's no but," Willow said quickly. "I don't want to date anyone I'm working with, and I'm hoping to continue construction with Griffin. If this case could just get solved, so the police would stop accusing Terry of the murder, we could focus on winning with Lady Valkyrie, and I could build my dog spa."

"Are you sure there's no story?"

"There's no story," Willow repeated. She was glad that they were on the phone so Wednesday couldn't see any traces of uncertainty on her face.

"All right." It sounded like her sister was pouting.

"I better go," Willow said, eager to end the call. "I have a lot to do. What with the championship, the construction, and the crime like I just mentioned."

"I guess I have a lot to do too. I need to figure something else out to focus on for 'My Life' today."

"Just don't forget about dinner with Dad tonight."

"Right," Wednesday said. Willow could practically hear the gears turning in her sister's head. "I wonder if that could be part of my feature. I wonder how photogenic Dad would be."

They said goodbye and hung up. Willow felt the urge to throw her phone across the room but refrained. There was nothing but bad news coming in today.

Telescope entered the kitchen and looked up at her.

"What terrible thing are you going to tell me now?" she accused the dog.

However, Telescope just wagged his tail.

"Sorry," she said, bending down close to him. "Maybe I'm overreacting."

He leaned against her, giving a doggie hug. She hugged him back, trying to calm herself. Why was Griffin meeting with Benny? What was he hoping to accomplish?

Willow's phone buzzed. She looked at Tele for support, then checked her text. Griffin was informing her that he was going to be late.

"Perfect," Willow muttered. "So, I've started this lousy day early for no reason."

She set the coffeemaker to begin another pot and then headed to the living room to sit in a more comfortable chair. While the coffee brewed in the kitchen, she stewed in her own thoughts. They weren't focused on Kaitlin's death but on Griffin's behavior. She couldn't figure it out.

She was sure Griffin didn't know Benny beforehand. She would have remembered if Griffin ever mentioned him, especially when she realized he was a suspect. If Griffin knew him, she wouldn't have had to go on a phony first date to question the businessman.

But, it hadn't ended up being a fake date. It had been fun and wonderful. It had left her wanting a second date.

Griffin had been pretty upset when she told him that she was going on a date. Did he follow her there? Had he been spying?

"I bet that's what it was," Willow said angrily.

Telescope was sitting on her lap and trying to comfort her. However, she was feeling more like a villain in an espionage thriller, stroking her pet's fur as she planned her nemesis's demise. If Griffin had been spying on her, she might not turn a laser weapon on him, but she would give him an earful as to what she thought about it.

This was why she wanted to keep her business and personal life separate. She didn't want romantic quarrels and jealousies bleeding into the workday. She didn't want her contractor following her around and scaring off potential rivals.

She wasn't sure how long she sat there brooding, but it must have been a while because Telescope fell asleep.

She woke him up with the proclamation. "I'm just going to have to lay down some ground rules. Griffin will have to know that it's all business when we're working on the dog spa."

Telescope licked her nose, and for once Willow wasn't sure what he meant. Was he being supportive or patronizing?

Or was she reading too much into her dog's reaction? She was tempted to ask him, but the pup fell asleep again.

She decided not to move and wake him again, so she continued to dwell on the same thoughts and felt herself growing more and more angry.

When the doorbell rang, she felt like a powder keg about to burst. However, she made sure to put on a bright smile when she greeted Griffin at the door.

"I'm sorry I'm late," he said while sporting his own smile.

"That's all right," Willow said pointedly. "I bet you needed to catch up on some sleep. Out late last night? Getting a few drinks?"

Griffin didn't seem to pick up on her tone. Instead, he revealed a paper bag that he had been hiding behind his back.

"I forgot what time the bakery on Sycamore opened. Most bakeries like to open at the crack of dawn, but Sycamore likes to take their sweet time in the morning."

Telescope wanted some attention and jumped onto his back leg. Griffin handed the bag over to Willow and knelt down to say hello. After scratching the dog's ears, he gave him a bone-shaped dog treat that also seemed fresh from the bakery.

All right, yes, it was nice that Griffin was starting to spoil her dog as much as she did, but it wasn't necessary. She did own a business that catered to canines. It wasn't like there was a shortage of treats to hand out. This was another example of things becoming too personal. She was going to have to set boundaries.

Telescope scooted off to either bury or eat his treat in peace. He gave Willow a look on his way that conveyed a warning not to overreact again. She knew she was probably going to ignore that advice.

"Pecan pie?"

"What?" she asked, turning her attention back to Griffin.

"I remembered you liked the Sycamore Street Bakery because they made muffin flavors that taste like pies. I thought pecan was your favorite, but I got some other flavors too."

The pecan pie muffin was her favorite, but now wasn't the time to admit that. She handed the bag of pastries back to Griffin.

"You don't have to buy me muffins."

A look of confusion crossed his face. "I thought you'd like them. You're always hungry in the morning."

Willow walked toward her kitchen to give her enough time to count to ten. Griffin closed the front door and followed her.

She gripped the counter as she spoke. "Griffin, I think we need to focus on business."

He was already taking out some coffee mugs and then began to pour the coffee. "Sure. You can tell me about any finishing touches you want at the dog gym, and the house only needs a little more work. It's just the aesthetics now. Do you want to change the trim color or something like that?"

"I want to talk about adding the doggie spa."

"You do expect to move forward with that?" he asked, pausing mid-pour.

"I do. I'm sure Terry will be cleared soon, and then we can focus on training. Lady Valkyrie is sure to win, and I'll have all the money needed for the extra renovations," she said, avoiding eye contact. "I thought the spa could branch out from my office since that's already used for business. It can take over the bathroom on the first floor. I know we'll have to expand the space too, and it would be easy to give up the hall closet. It might have to extend into my current living room, especially if I keep having Great Danes as customers."

"It would probably take up at least half of your living room if you want the wall to run straight from your office."

"I can live with that," she said, finally accepting a cup of coffee from him.

"Willow, are you sure you want to do this?"

"What do you mean? Of course, I want to."

He played with his mug. "It just doesn't seem like your heart is really in this. You're an amazing dog trainer. But the one time I was here, and you bathed Tele, we both ended up soaking wet. And he's chihuahua."

"Chihuahua-mix."

Griffin joined her at the counter. "I think maybe it's like being a contractor and an interior designer. They're similar, but not the same. I think you might be trying to force something because it seems like a good idea on paper. But is it really the right thing for you?"

"Are you a contractor and a therapist now?" she asked, walking away.

"I didn't mean to upset you," he said earnestly.

"It is a good idea on paper, and it's a great idea in real life to become a one-stop place for your dogs," Willow said, crossing her arms. "I don't know why you're trying to undermine this. But I guess that's becoming a habit for you."

"What do you mean by that?" Griffin asked, setting his coffee down a little harder than was necessary.

"Forget it. I want to focus on *business*. I want to focus on the spa."

"Are you sure?" he asked again.

Willow's eyes narrowed. "What? Are you trying to get out of your contract?"

Griffin sighed. "That's not... Well, I did think this project was almost over. And I do have another offer. But I wouldn't say I'm trying to get out of my contract."

"You are," Willow said, grabbing a muffin and shaking it. "These muffins were a bribe."

"No," he said, picking one but holding it like an offering. "They were celebratory muffins."

"What are we celebrating?" Willow asked, setting down her pastry before she reduced it to crumbs.

"Well, I thought we were celebrating that your house was almost done and that I got an offer for an amazing new project, and..." He continued talking but it was mumbled as if it embarrassed him. All Willow could make out was the word "dating" and she decided to jump on it.

"Dating?" she asked. "Like how you tried to crash my date last night?"

"What are you talking about?"

Willow hated that he was playing dumb. "Wednesday saw you with Benny after I left."

"That's who you had your date with?"

"You didn't know?"

"I had a business meeting with Benny Gene last night," Griffin said, shaking his head. "We were discussing a new project over drinks. He wants me to do the renovations for his consulting job. It's a great opportunity for me."

Willow couldn't think of anything to say at first. Griffin mistakenly took this as a good sign and that it was safe to tell her the details of the project.

"It would be a great resume builder because I haven't done much with hotels. And it should get a fair amount of press because Benny wants to use it to boost his consulting opportunities as well." He looked down as he admitted, "I'd really like to take the job."

Willow didn't know how to feel. She felt a decent amount of rage directed towards both men. Benny had double-booked the night of their date, and Griffin was looking for other jobs instead of finishing her spa. Both of these things felt like a betrayal.

A small part of her was relieved that Griffin was there for a business meeting. He wasn't spying on her. He also wasn't on a date like she had briefly feared when she saw him at the restaurant.

She pushed that thought away. She wasn't interested in Griffin romantically. Not as long as they were working together.

"Well, this is great," Willow said, choosing to direct her anger at the person who was in front of her. "You're throwing me over for a new client. Thanks for the muffins. It's just as good as finishing the business I wanted to build."

Griffin threw his arms up. "I'm not throwing you over for anyone. In fact, well, you're the person I care most about."

"You have a funny way of showing it," Willow challenged.

"I am interested in this other job," Griffin said. "But there are some other factors that make me hesitant to jump into shrinking your living room and making a spa. Firstly, I don't want you to overextend yourself on a project you can't currently afford."

"So, it's all about the money?" Willow asked. She knew that wasn't fair but didn't care at the moment.

"The other reason I'm hesitant is because I really wanted to ask you on a date, and I was pretty sure you'd say no while we were still renovating together."

Willow froze. She didn't think this was something that they would ever admit to each other.

"Well," she said, finding her voice, "I would have said no. I don't date people I'm working with."

"I don't get it," Griffin said. He took her empty mug and his and put them in the sink.

"Get what?"

"If two people like each other, they should be able to date," he said as he washed the mugs.

Willow put her hands on her hips. "You don't think there will inevitably be complications?"

"I think people can be professional and in love at the same time," he said evenly.

"Well, I think that one person will inevitable try and use the other person. Romantic fights will lead to bad business decisions. Everything could become compromised. I can see why businesses have policies against it," Willow said. "Maybe you should add a page about that to your employee handbook."

"Why are you determined to fight today?" Griffin asked, turning off the water and throwing down the sponge.

"Maybe it had something to do with you quitting my job and ending up in cahoots with my date."

"Look, if you want me to do the spa, I will. I don't break contracts, and I won't leave you in the lurch," he said, pointing for emphasis. "However, I can't help my feelings. This is where I stand. I want to build Benny's buildings, and I want to date you."

Willow moved to the other side of the island counter. "I don't think I stand in the same place. I like things how they are."

Griffin nodded and looked down.

"And besides," Willow said, "I might have just started seeing someone."

"You don't mean Benny?" Griffin asked, meeting her eyes. "He said the date was a bust."

"Oh, like I'd believe that from you." She crossed her arms, feeling the anger build again.

"It's not a trick. It's what he said. I just didn't realize he was talking about you at the time."

Willow scoffed instead of dignifying that with an answer.

"He said he wasn't interested in anything long-term with you. He said you asked too many questions. He thought you might get clingy."

"Clingy? Do I seem clingy?"

"No," Griffin said. "I'm embarrassed to tell you all this, but I think you should know. He said he was willing to sleep with you, but you wouldn't bite."

"You're just trying to get me mad, so I won't want to see him again," Willow said.

"Did he tell you a story about his dog that saved his life when he was a kid? And it was in a wheelchair?"

"Yes," she admitted.

"That was a line. He said that he told you that story because he knew you loved dogs, and he was hoping you'd suggest that you should go his hotel room."

"No," Willow said, not wanting to believe it.

"Did he keep mentioning that the place he was staying at was close by?"

"Well…" She trailed off as she realized it was true. So, it hadn't been the perfect first date she thought it was! Benny was the *real* dog in the story.

"I'm sorry," Griffin said.

"I knew it was just a hookup app," Willow grumbled.

She tapped the counter, annoyed with Benny and herself. She really thought that they had chemistry and that more dates could have followed. Benny had been lying all night. Then, a more sinister thought entered her head. Benny could have been lying about a lot more than having a dog. What if he really was involved in Kaitlin's death?

13

W illow arrived on her father's doorstep with a bottle of wine promptly at six o'clock for their weekly family meal. Earlier in the day, she had been worried that her side of the dinner table conversation would keep veering towards how she couldn't believe her father could suspect Terry Gib.

Now, she had so much on her mind that she didn't think she'd be able to form a coherent accusation. She hoped that Wednesday would be able to keep the chatter going and compensate for her distraction.

She opened the door and announced her arrival. Her dad called to her from the kitchen. She walked in and was greeted by the succulent smell of rosemary chicken and potatoes.

"Do you need any help?" Willow asked, after placing her

wine in the fridge. She glanced around the room. With its checkered blue wallpaper, it looked exactly the same as it did when she was growing up. The only slight differences were the electric appliances on the counter. They had been updated at some point down the line.

"All that's left is to bring the food to the dining room table," Frank said.

"Should we wait for Wednesday?"

"Wednesday is not coming," he said as he sliced the chicken and placed it on a serving plate.

"What?"

"She sent me a text," he said matter-of-factly. "It was full of emojis, but I gathered that she wasn't going to make it because she needed to focus on her life."

Willow groaned, but then sensing her father's agitation as well, she stood up for her sister. "When she says she's focusing on her *life*, she means the social media assignment that's due this week. Not her life in general."

"I know," he said, continuing to carve.

"Do you want me to read the text and explain the pictures?"

"I've been deciphering her texts for years," Frank said. "Luckily, I've been a detective for many years too. Let's go and eat."

He picked up the chicken and headed out of the kitchen.

Willow was about to grab a side dish but decided to text her sister before she went to the dining room. Her message of

"Why did you bail on us?" was replied to with a picture of Wednesday enjoying a solo picnic in the park. Admittedly, with her sister's filters and eye for layout, it looked like a fantastic evening out. However, this didn't help the fact that Willow would now have to be the social only child that night.

She and her father finished setting the table. Frank was setting every food dish down with extra restraint, treating each bowl as if it were a flower. Willow couldn't disguise her negative feelings towards the world and was letting the silverware plop down into place.

They took their seats and Willow said, "It looks delicious, Dad."

"I'm glad you're here to enjoy it."

She nodded and started to fill her plate. However, despite how good it all looked, her mind wasn't on the meal. She was thinking about how complicated things had become suddenly. It seemed that somebody had snuck into Kaitlin's house and poisoned her coffee grounds, and the suspect list seemed to be growing. It now included the sweet date of hers who was really a liar.

It wasn't just the murder that was complicated either. Her instincts seemed completely off these days. She had been wrong about Benny. She also hadn't realized Griffin's level of attraction to her. She knew that they were friends, and that there was the potential that something was simmering beneath the surface, but she didn't expect either of them to act on it.

Part of her wished her dad would just ask her what was

wrong so that she could get everything off her chest. Her feelings were suffocating her, and she was finding it difficult to enjoy the chicken.

"Can you pass the peas, please?" Willow asked.

Frank picked the dish up roughly but then handed it to her with the utmost care. She smiled in thanks and piled peas on her plate. Then she let the bowl hit the table with a thud. Her dad didn't say anything. He was sighing into his mashed potatoes.

Willow chewed for a few minutes and decided that maybe her chair not being in a good spot was causing some of her distraction. She adjusted her seat forward and back, trying to find the right spot.

Frank had begun tapping on his plate with his fork and frowning. Willow stopped moving her chair and started to consider whether something was bothering her dad besides Wednesday standing them up.

"Is everything all right?"

"Well," Frank said, and Willow could tell that he had been waiting for her to ask. However, "No" was all the response she got at first.

"What's wrong?"

Her dad seemed to be debating what to say but then finally pointed his fork towards Wednesday's empty chair.

"I don't like that she's not here either," Willow said. "And maybe we would have liked to be invited on her picnic? Then again, I think I might have shared as much of my life as I'd like to with her followers."

She realized that she was rambling and stopped so her dad could talk.

"I'm happy that her Instagramming is going well. I really am. But that doesn't mean that she can drop the ball in other aspects of her life."

Willow bit her lip. "Is she not doing all the paperwork that's she's supposed to be doing?"

"I know police secretary might not be the most glamorous job, but it is what pays her bills right now. The internet didn't pay for her cat's stitches."

It occurred to Willow that Wednesday probably could have gotten some followers to donate to a "Save the Tail" campaign, but she silenced the thought.

"But more than that," Frank said, "the work is important. Paperwork might be boring, and I know there's a lot of it during review week, but this is what makes the station run smoothly. Her work makes sure that we can fulfill our duty to protect and serve. And usually she's amazing at it. But she's been so distracted lately. Of course, when I try to tell her all this, she thinks that I'm merely obsessing over my bio that she has to write."

"Are you obsessing over the bio?" Willow asked, poking at her meal.

"Not obsessing," he said. He began to pick at his food too. "I suppose, like my youngest daughter, I do care about the image of me that is presented to the world. I don't want my life story slapped together haphazardly in a few minutes."

She looked up at him and said honestly, "I'm sure Wednesday will write an accurate bio for you that shows what an incredible police chief you are. It might even say that you're a great dad too."

He nodded, and she knew that he was touched by what she said. Her dad wasn't always great at expressing his emotions. He wasn't often so open when talking about his life. Most of their conversations growing up had been about possible solutions to fictitious (and sometimes actual cold case) crimes, preparing her to become a detective. The detective thing hadn't quite worked out. Though she had solved one case since being back in town and now did find herself looking into a poisoning.

"Thanks," Frank said, directing his attention to his plate. "I'm not quite sure about the incredible police chief part."

"What do you mean?"

"Gathering up the information for my bio has me looking through old cases. I can see all the mistakes I've made through the years. Some more recent than others. Maybe Wednesday had noticed them too."

"Dad, if Wednesday noticed something, she would tell you. She's not someone who keeps her opinion to herself. And she's definitely not avoiding work because she wants to write that you've been terrible at your job. That can't be true. She's distracted by this campaign. But I'll talk to her and remind her about other things going on in *her life*."

Frank gave a slight nod. "Are you finished eating?"

Willow agreed that she was, and they brought the dishes into the kitchen. Frank began putting the leftovers away while she loaded the dishwasher.

"Was something bothering you too?"

"Well," Willow said, balancing some plates, "what would be less awkward for you to hear about: my feelings towards you investigating my champion dog's owner or boy troubles?"

Frank froze, and she couldn't help laughing at the expression on his face.

"Forget it," Willow said. "There's not much to say on either end. I seem to have terrible taste with the men I actually date. Or marry. And the one that you do like... Never mind."

"You can tell me," Frank said, valiantly resuming his tasks. "I'm your father. I want to help you in any way I can. Even this."

Accepting the invitation to talk, Willow said, "I thought I was ready to start dating again, but it's all been so complicated. And the person who is complicating it the most... well, I thought it would be like high school again. We'd feel there was something special to our friendship, but we wouldn't do anything about it. That way we wouldn't have to deal with any consequences. I also really don't want to date anyone I'm doing business with. It turned out really badly last time."

Frank seemed to ponder this. "I'm not good explaining

this sort of thing. But when I started dating your mom, it felt right. And I bet that will happen for you too." Then, after clearing his throat, he added, "And if anyone ever gives you trouble, you can remind him that your father is the Chief of Police."

She grinned. "Thanks, Dad."

Frank had stopped smiling after he said that though.

"If you're worried about me bringing up the murder case, there's not much to say," she assured him as she finished with the dishes. "I don't think Terry was involved. But I don't have any evidence against someone else. All I know are some potential motives."

Frank nodded sadly. "I was waiting for you to bring it up."

"That Terry is innocent?"

"Those potential motives," Frank said. "You're talking about Linda Grego, aren't you?"

"Linda?" Willow repeated. She remembered Linda making comments to Wednesday after yoga, but she didn't know anything that would cause this reaction in her father.

"My most recent mistake," he admitted, as he placed the final lid on a piece of Tupperware. "All those complaints she made about the victim's bed-and-breakfast – I ignored them."

"I know a little about this," she said, moving closer. "What were the complaints about?"

"She was trying to get the B&B's license revoked. She wanted it closed down for health violations."

"Isn't that place pristine though?" Willow asked. "It's won

awards, and I've never heard a negative review from anyone staying there."

"The guest area was kept very clean," Frank said, nodding. "But Kaitlin Janes's personal quarters weren't. That might be what the complaints were in regard to. It seems the victim was a hoarder."

"I wouldn't have expected that."

Like so much else in this case, this new information seemed contradictory. Kaitlin had a spotless B&B but was a hoarder and slob at home. Also, if the guests never saw Kaitlin's personal quarters, why would someone work so hard on a complaint against the establishment? Maybe there was another reason why Linda wanted it closed down. Maybe she wanted to hurt Kaitlin, and when her attempts to kill the business failed, she went after the business owner.

"There was a lot of her personal property that we needed to process. That took a while," Frank said. "But it helped us out in one regard. We were able to find traces of poison in coffee mugs all around the apartment."

"Well, that's it," Willow said, wanting to clap and voice her suspicions at the same time. "You have a prime suspect. Linda wanted the place closed down. She could have snuck into Kaitlin's apartment and poisoned the coffee grounds."

Frank shook his head. "We did consider her. We found her business card attached to one of Kaitlin's bags of coffee."

"That sounds like evidence to me."

"However, the coffee grounds weren't poisoned. The

poison was poured into her cup of coffee. And it must have happened multiple times for it to build up in her system. We couldn't place Linda Grego at the bed-and-breakfast in the morning when the victim was drinking the coffee, so we had to dismiss her as a suspect. Beyond those complaints, there was no motive."

Willow nodded, but she was deep in thought. The coffee itself was poisoned and not the grounds? That would make this murder more difficult to execute. However, it certainly didn't sound like Linda Grego minded extra steps when making a complaint. Maybe it was the same with murder?

Willow would just have to check and see if she could prove that Linda had snuck over to the B&B in the morning.

"Do you want dessert?" Frank asked, taking out a batch of chocolate chip cookies.

Willow nodded. She deserved a cookie after making a potential break in the case.

14

Back home and dressed in her most comfortable pajamas, a matching top and bottom with a pattern of sleeping puppies curled up into balls, Willow wandered into her living room. She had a glass of wine in one hand and was trying to decompress. She took a sip and decided that her ten-dollar bottle was actually much better than the stuff that Benny had ordered on their date. Or was that just sour grapes?

She swirled her drink and sighed. It wasn't just finding out that Benny wasn't the perfect date that bothered her, (though his lying could have ramifications for him as a suspect.) No, it was that she hadn't seen through his act. After everything that she had been through with her ex, she thought she was smarter. She thought she was better at seeing others' ulterior motives and knew what she wanted out of a relationship now.

However, she had been misled again. Maybe she really wasn't ready to date.

She looked at the one male who had never let her down to see if he had any words of advice, but Telescope was snoozing on the couch, looking like the cuddly design on her PJs.

Getting no response but puppy snores, Willow turned her attention to the rest of the room. She placed a hand on the wall and then tried to imagine what it would look like if it were cut in half. Griffin was right; she would be losing a lot of personal space.

She felt doubts about the dog spa creeping into her head. It would mean more business, but that would also mean more work. Griffin was also right when he said that he thought she preferred training to grooming. She did like seeing a dog reach his potential athletically and with understanding what a trainer was communicating. She much preferred that to covering a canine in suds and getting herself soaked in the process. To compensate, would she have to cut back on the part of her job that she loved?

She took another sip of wine and tried to quell these concerns. She had already hired some employees. She could hire more if she expanded as well. With the other grooming place in town closing, opening her own made business sense.

And yet she was having nagging concerns about losing this room. She would be sacrificing her personal space for her business. It wasn't a big deal right now, but could it be down the line? She was thinking of Pineview as her forever home and was planning on staying in this house. What if she wanted to start a family someday? She would want the downstairs bathroom and the extra living room space then.

She realized she was pacing and then tried to imagine this movement in the smaller living room. She groaned as she considered that Griffin could be right again. Was she trying to force this build because it looked good on paper? Was she not considering the other consequences?

Of course, if she did stop these renovations, Griffin wouldn't be a part of her life like he had been. Their morning coffee meetings where they joked and talked about life under the guise of construction plans would be a thing of the past. She hated to admit it but seeing Griffin for those talks made her not hate the mornings. Sometimes she even enjoyed waking up early.

However, she couldn't be doing all this for a cup of coffee in the morning, could she? Would she really miss seeing Griffin that much?

She hit the wall with her palm and heard a slight thud.

If that were the case, she might as well date Griffin like he suggested. Of course, that was terrifying. She wanted to start *dating* – not to jump into a relationship that could lead to commitment. That wasn't what she wanted.

"What I need," Willow said aloud, "is more wine."

She followed her own advice and refilled her glass. Then, she cuddled up next to Telescope on the couch and turned on the television. She wanted to turn off her brain, but she couldn't help noticing that her TV was partially in the area that would have to be given up for the dog spa.

She drank a little more and flipped through the channels.

"What do you feel like watching?" she asked the dog. Telescope had opened his eyes but seemed to shrug in reply.

She settled on a Lifetime thriller and eventually found herself focusing on the characters' troubles instead of her own. She could usually figure out the ending of this type of movie pretty early on, but they were fun to watch.

"Aha!" Willow said, struggling not to spill her drink in her enthusiasm to solve the movie's mystery. "They want us to think it's the football player, but it's really his little brother. He's the one who had access to the jacket the witness saw."

Telescope wagged his tail. Willow leaned back to see if she was right.

"If only I could figure out what happened to Kaitlin so easily," she muttered.

Tele moved closer, and she petted him as she thought about the murder. Her father told her that the coffee was poisoned but not the grounds. Who would have been able to poison what was in Kaitlin's mug between when she poured it and when she finished drinking it? And who could have done this daily until she died?

Because of their former relationship, Kaitlin would probably have admitted Jack into her house. Would she have let Benny or Linda inside her apartment? Would they be able to sneak inside and add the poison if she didn't let them in?

Linda had been making complaints about the B&B, and Benny wanted to buy it. Would that have given them insider information on how to break into her house unobserved?

It became clear that she was right about the thriller on TV, but she still didn't have any more answers about her mystery.

She picked up the phone, looking for something else to distract her. She hadn't checked on Wednesday's posts for the day yet and decided to scroll through them. It would be nice to see what her sister was up to when she wasn't including Willow's dating life.

At first, Willow enjoyed looking at the pictures. They were fun and got lots of likes. There were pictures of Wednesday curling her hair while her cat watched, grilling paninis, and climbing the trees in the park. There were also some shots of her riding go-carts and then volunteering at a soup kitchen.

When she reached the pictures of the picnic, Willow frowned. By the amount of posts and locations she saw, it looked as if Wednesday was never at work. No wonder her father was worried. How much paperwork could Wednesday get done while she was roller skating?

She sent her sister a text reminding her that their dad was anxious about the bio she was supposed to write but didn't get a response right away. Willow hoped that Wednesday was doing some work for her job, or she might not have it to come back to once this *week* was done.

After receiving no reply and not wanting to add any more "likes," Willow looked for something else to play with on her phone. Another thriller was beginning on TV, (this time Willow suspected the mother) and she found herself clicking on Tinder.

She sipped her wine and started swiping through potential matches. No one was jumping out at her. Was she being too picky? Was she being a chicken? Was she being smart? She answered herself with a big gulp of rosé and kept swiping.

Then, she saw a picture that made her pause. Griffin's face was staring at her from her screen. He looked just as he did in person. She could make out the shadow of his muscular arms and the unique shade of his piercing blue eyes.

She gulped. Which way should she swipe for Griffin? She had to admit an attraction, and she did love their morning coffee chats. However, they were still working together.

She felt silly as she noticed her hand was trembling.

"Too much wine," she muttered instead of acknowledging that being forced to make a decision was frightening.

Telescope nudged her hand. Willow nodded. She was going to make a choice. Any minute now she was going to make a choice. She just needed to move her thumb. She just needed to swipe the picture. But which way? Left or right?

Heart in her throat and wine in her hand, she swiped right. She exhaled a deep breath.

The answer was immediate. They were a match!

15

"Where is it?" Willow muttered as she scoured her house looking for the shade of lipstick that was hiding on her. She knew that Griffin had seen her during her awkward high school days and when she was only half-awake before the coffee was brewed while they started working together. However, if she was going to do this dating thing, she was going to do it right. That included throwing some lipstick on.

After checking the normal hiding spots, she started searching in some more unusual ones. However, when she started digging through Telescope's treat bag, she realized that she was becoming desperate.

Telescope bounded into the room when he heard the crinkle of the bag.

She turned to him with hands on her hips. "Did you hide it on me?"

He barked, and she gave him a snack so it wouldn't seem like she was teasing him. After he finished eating, he headed back to the front door. He seemed to know that someone was about to arrive.

Willow sighed. She couldn't think where else to look and searching for her missing tube was the one thing that had been distracting her from overanalyzing her decision to go on this date. She felt a different sort of nervousness from when she went on her other Tinder date. With Benny, she hadn't been expecting much because her main reason to chat with him was to determine if was a killer. (The jury was still out on that call.) It had also seemed safe because Benny was based in New York City and only traveled here for business. A relationship like that could be casual and comfortable. She didn't want a booty call, but she also wasn't ready to jump right into a major commitment.

She checked the time. She knew Griffin liked to arrive early for appointments. Would it be the same for dates? If so, then she only had a few more minutes to push off her panic attack and decide on an alternate shade of gloss.

She double-checked that she hadn't left her lipstick in the bathroom and reminded herself, "Just stick to the plan."

The plan was to keep the prospect of a first date from becoming too terrifying. To do that, she would do the same thing that she did on her last date. She would try and interview a suspect at the same time. This time her target was Linda. And she had an idea on how to run into her.

She chuckled to herself as she realized that she found talking to a murder suspect less intimidating than a date with a handsome and kind man. The doorbell rang, accompanied by Telescope's cheerful barks. Her date had arrived.

She opened the door to see Griffin in a blue button-down shirt that complemented his eyes and found herself saying, "You clean up good, kid."

Out of construction boots, it was certainly true. However, she couldn't help cringing that those were the first words out of her mouth on their date. Why did she call him kid?

"I guess most of the time you see me I'm sweaty, and my clothes are covered in paint and dust," he said with a laugh.

Willow refrained from commenting on how attractive he could be then too, with his sleeves rolled up to show his firm arm muscles. Instead, she focused on the flowers in his hand.

"Are those for me?"

"Nah. They're for Tele," he teased before handing them over.

"They're beautiful," she said, looking at them. "But, am I – was I supposed to get you something too? I might be rusty at this."

"Will, relax. Just be yourself," Griffin said. "And besides, I'm a contractor. I know how to deal with rust."

She groaned at the joke and headed further into her house. She quickly placed the flowers in a vase and grabbed her purse. She returned to see Griffin petting Tele. He stood up and smiled when he saw her.

"I'm all ready," she said, digging into her purse for her keys and finding her missing lipstick. How could she have forgotten to check there? It was right under her nose the whole time. "Actually, give me five seconds."

She used the hall mirror to apply the lipstick and then walked to the door.

"Have I told you yet that you look beautiful?" Griffin asked.

Telescope barked and they both looked at him.

Willow smiled. "He said I better be home by curfew or else."

"Don't worry," Griffin said to the pup. "I'll take good care of her."

Telescope seemed appeased, and the two humans left and headed for Griffin's truck.

"I'm really excited about the bar we chose to eat at," he said. "Having so many craft beers on tap sounds amazing. I looked it up after you told me about it. They have over a hundred."

"I know. It's like a unicorn in wine country," Willow agreed. "But, you know, I'm not quite hungry yet. Would you mind if we took a detour before dinner?"

"Not at all. What did you have in mind?"

"There's a farmers' market in town," Willow suggested.

"They have a lot of local stands, and we can see what they have to offer."

Griffin agreed, saying it was perfect weather to wander around the tables.

Willow smiled. It was easier to convince him to go there than she thought it would be. She did love visiting the farmers' market for fresh fruits and vegetables. However, it wasn't tomatoes or watermelon that Willow was looking for today. It was Linda Grego.

Linda was involved in many town activities, and Willow was pretty sure she had heard her mention that she had a stand at the farmers' market while she was at the dog gym. She remembered Linda trying to convince Shelly to come buy her homemade candles.

They parked outside the market and headed in together. Some of the vendors were beginning to closeup shop, but others were staying late to catch people when they got off work.

She hoped that Linda would still be there. She knew that her father had dismissed Linda as a suspect, but Willow felt like she needed to get her own read on her. Terry had been told not to leave town, and it was sounding like the case against her was gathering steam.

Despite the secrets that Terry had kept from her at first, Willow didn't think that she was the killer. She couldn't believe that Terry would poison somebody. Also, why would Terry have suggested that Willow look into Jack as a potential killer before the death was ruled a murder? Surely, the killer wanted this to be ruled a natural death, so they could get away with the crime. It didn't make sense for the killer to accuse someone when it looked like an illness.

Someone else had killed Kaitlin and was allowing Terry to take the blame. Willow was going to find out who it was. She didn't want her friend to go down for a crime she didn't commit.

Plus, once all the chaos had died down, they would be able to focus on training for the dog competition again. She knew that all three of them (dog included) could really use a win.

Willow wandered ahead, trying to find Linda's table.

"I only have eyes for you," Griffin said.

That made Willow stop abruptly. It was certainly a forward thing to say on a first date even if they were friends. She turned towards him, ready to tell him to cool his jets but ended up bursting out laughing. He was holding up two potatoes and grinning.

"If you keep making those jokes, you're going to get an earful," Willow challenged, picking up an ear of corn and jabbing it towards him.

"That's pretty corny," he countered.

"If you think that's bad..." Willow trailed off as she saw the stand she was looking for. "Candles."

She set the corn down and headed off towards the table.

"Hey," Griffin said, following. "Where are you *stalking* off to?"

He was soon at her side. They approached the table, but Willow was unhappy to see that there was no one there. She picked up a candle and peered around. Griffin started sniffing the candles.

"This one's nice," he said, offering it to her to smell.

Willow nodded in agreement.

"That's my pomegranate honey candle. Very popular," Linda said, running up to the table. "In fact, I just had to get another box of them."

"It's a crowd favorite?" Griffin asked.

She nodded. Then, she recognized Willow. "Hello there. Looking for something sweet to cover up the smell of your dogs? I love to use these around my house if Pattie ever has wet fur."

"That's a good idea," Willow said, picking up another candle and twirling it in her hands. "There are lots of times that you might want to cover up the scent of a dirty dog. Did they use these at the dog-friendly B&B in town?"

"This is just a hobby for me right now because of the time constraints from my job, so I only sell them at the farmers' market. I am trying to expand but haven't yet. I don't think Kaitlin ever came to my table," she said with a shrug.

Griffin raised an eyebrow at the mention of the victim's name.

"And I suppose now she can't. I wasn't thinking," Willow said, frowning. "It's a shame what happened to her."

"It is. But it's not all that surprising," Linda said. "Maybe if the city had responded to my complaints, this might not have happened. They could have cited her for not storing the rat poison properly. Though, I'm not one to gossip."

Another customer came up to the table, inquiring, "Did you get that other box of candles?"

Linda turned her attention to the eager woman who wanted to buy her wares. It looked like she might take a while. Griffin gestured with his head, and Willow followed him away from the table.

"Sorry," she said.

"Don't be," he said with a smile. "We became close again when you were investigating Lee Hunter's murder. I should have expected there would be some carryover."

"I have to help Terry if I can," Willow said.

"Well, we made a pretty good team last time."

Willow smiled in agreement and asked him what he thought about Linda. "The way she talked – it didn't sound personal. It sounded matter-of-fact."

"If she knew Kaitlin was going to die, maybe it was matter-of-fact for her."

Willow nodded thoughtfully.

"Any other vegetables you want to check out? Or suspects? Either one you want to grill?"

"No," Willow said, giving him a smile. "I'd like to go to dinner with you now. And I promise not to do any more investigating tonight."

"Uh oh," Willow said as they entered Tapped.

"What?" Griffin joked. "Are they out of one beer? Will we only have ninety-nine options to choose from?"

"No," she said, scrunching her face up. "It's that someone is here."

She pointed across the bar to where Benny was talking to another man.

"Your ex," Griffin teased. But then he said, "If you're embarrassed, we don't have to stay."

"Part of the reason why I even went out with him was because I thought he might have been a suspect in Kaitlin's death. Now, I think he might be again."

Griffin crossed his arms and gave her a look. "Was our entire date an excuse to interrogate people?"

"No," Willow said earnestly. "If I wanted you as backup, I would have just asked. I didn't know Benny would be here. Admittedly, I did learn about this place from him. But I didn't know he'd be here tonight."

Benny must have noticed them when they came in because he walked over with his companion in tow.

"Griffin Maynard, what are the odds of seeing you here?" Benny asked, exuding charm. "Maybe it's fate. Have you decided to take on my hotel project?"

"Well, um, it certainly is tempting," Griffin said, casting a glance at Willow. "But I'm still deciding."

Benny seemed to finally notice who was accompanying his potential contractor.

"Hello, Benny," Willow said with a big smile.

"Hi," Benny said, matching it. "You know, I've been meaning to message you. Sadly, I've been busy with work. It appears I might have missed my opportunity with you."

"It's a shame too. I did want to hear more about your poor dog, Rufus," Willow said.

"Good old Rufus," Benny said, placing a hand on his heart.

"Or was it Roscoe?" Willow asked, tapping her chin.

"I'm Griffin," Griffin said quickly, extending his hand to the fourth member of their party.

"Curt," was the response.

"Curt here is the concierge at the hotel I'm consulting with now," Benny explained. "I'm pumping him for all the dirt on the place."

Curt laughed.

"You're a concierge?" Willow asked, turning her attention to him. "Do you run some sort of running concierge service?"

"She remembered. She's a really good listener," Benny said. Then, he leaned in towards Griffin and whispered, "Be careful with that."

"I do *run* that service," Curt said. "I lead the guests and some locals that like to join in on a jogging tour of some nearby scenic areas."

"And Benny has been joining in?" Willow asked.

"Really careful," Benny repeated quietly to Griffin after giving her a suspicious look.

"All week," Curt said. "He's been on all my tours."

"I've been testing out the amenities offered," Benny said. "I think that is a successful offering."

"And you two have been together every morning?" Willow asked.

"Yes. He was there all morning—" Curt started to say.

"Hotel concierges are hired to be discreet," Benny said, keeping his smile. "He's not going to tell you if I had any late-night visitors."

Willow laughed. "You caught me."

"But I'm interested in this running concierge business," Griffin said, trying to keep the conversation going. "Where do you run?"

"Different locations around here and the surrounding towns."

"Do you ever go near Pineview?" Griffin asked. "That's where I live. I might want to join in."

"We go through Pineview somedays. Down Main Street."

"Were you running there the day that lady was murdered?" Griffin asked as if the terrible idea had just occurred to him.

"That's right!" Curt said. "It was a normal run day. Mr. Gene and I were going to lead a tour. We had to wait because a large family had signed up to join us and were running late. However, we did our run down Main Street. Then, we saw this woman walking her dog. She looked funny and started to fall over. Mr. Gene was the closet. He caught her, but it was too late for us to do anything. She was dead. An ambulance came. We thought it was a heart attack or something. It wasn't until I read it in the local paper that I learned that she was killed with rat poison and the police were looking at it as a murder."

"Discretion," Benny repeated.

Curt looked abashed. "Sorry, Mr. Gene."

Willow wanted to tell him not to be so hard on the concierge. He had just provided an alibi for Benny. If he was with the jogging group all week, he couldn't have snuck away to poison Kaitlin's coffee multiple mornings. It also would have been impossible for him to do it the day that she actually died because the run had started late.

"I wonder what's going to happen to that bed-and-breakfast," Griffin said. "I mean, I wonder if the new owner will need a contractor."

"If you sign on with me for my hotel project, you can have the B&B one too," Benny said. "If it's local projects that you like."

"You're going to buy it?" Willow asked.

Benny nodded as if that were obvious. "I'll put a bid in as soon as it goes on sale. I'd been interested in the property for a while. It might be difficult to overcome the murder in marketing, but it is a nice building. If we can't keep dog owners coming there, we might be able to do some ghostly promotions in the fall. Something for Halloween."

"It sounds like you've been thinking about this a lot," Willow said.

"As soon as the ambulance took her away, I had the idea," Benny said. "It's a good one, isn't it? I bet we could get some customers in the door if they think they might actually see something spooky."

All Willow found creepy was how quickly Benny had been able to spin a woman's death into something profitable. She wasn't even cold in the ground. Her murder wasn't even solved yet. Benny was clearly the heartless shark of a businessman she had pegged him as before their date.

Even though she had lost most of her appetite, she said that she and Griffin really needed to get some dinner. They asked to be seated and began looking over the large beer list.

"I hope that was helpful," Griffin said, as he smiled at her over his menu.

"It was," Willow said. "In more than one way."

Even though she found his business practices despicable, Willow had ruled Benny out as a suspect in the murder. She had also never felt luckier to be out with an honest and genuinely nice man.

As she and Griffin made puns about the flavors of beer they could order, reminisced about high school days, and shared their suspicious, Willow couldn't help thinking that this was her new favorite first date.

16

"Remind me why we're doing this again?" Willow said. It was the afternoon after her wonderful date, and yet she and her sister were leaving her car and heading towards the building that housed Jack's dating coach office.

"You think you're such an expert in dating now that you don't need any more help?" Wednesday challenged. "Did things go that well with Griffin? Are you off the market now?"

"No," Willow said, holding her hands up. "I mean, like I told you, it was a great date."

"Yeah, yeah. You ruled out one suspect and became more suspicious of another," Wednesday said, rolling her eyes. "Real romantic."

"We had some great beer."

Wednesday still looked unimpressed. Willow had given

her sister the details of her date, but somehow couldn't articulate how wonderful it had been. Being with Griffin, whether it was while tricking suspects into revealing information or just holding hands at the end of the night, felt right.

"You were the one who was rooting for us to get together," Willow said.

"And I still want you to," Wednesday said. "It just doesn't sound like you're really together yet. So, I think you should explore other options too."

"You just want more pictures for your 'Week in My Life.'"

"That's an added plus," she admitted.

"Speaking of your life," Willow said, trying to make a segue. "Are there any pictures of you doing paperwork at your office in your roll? Maybe writing Dad's bio?"

"Look, we're here," Wednesday said, neatly sidestepping the question and pointing to the door. "Do you want to take Jack up on his generous offer to give you another session free of charge? Or should we blow him off?"

Willow opened the door, indicating that they would go inside. Because Jack hadn't asked to see her alone, she knew he most likely made the offer to meet with her again for the social media likes Wednesday could get him and not out of the kindness of his heart. However, Willow was okay with that. She planned on using this session to get some answers to some lingering questions she had about his relationship with Kaitlin.

"Ladies," Jack said with arms open wide as they entered the room. He hugged Wednesday. Willow was surprised by this reaction. She was even more surprised when Jack hugged her as well. She awkwardly patted his back.

He released her and gave her an appraising look. "An awkward hugger. We're going to have to work on that."

"I'm not an awkward hugger," Willow protested. "I just need to know the person I'm hugging."

Jack shrugged as if he didn't believe her. "Your sister is an excellent hugger. You should take some pointers from her."

Willow opened her mouth to object again, but Wednesday beat her to it.

"You really think my hugs are excellent?" she asked.

He nodded, and then the two of them took some selfies demonstrating the art of the hug. Willow waited not-so-patiently.

"I'm glad I came in for my dating consult," she said.

"I'm sorry," Jack said. "My passion and enthusiasm get away from me sometimes. I won't say that's something to emulate all the time, but sometimes it does keep your partner interested."

"It's all right," Willow said. "I've actually been doing well with dating recently."

"Because of the advice I gave you?" Jack said, accepting the compliment before she gave it.

"Sure," Willow said, to keep him in a good mood so he would want to answer her questions later.

"She's been on two dates," Wednesday reported.

"That's right," Willow said. "I set up a Tinder account."

"With my help," Wednesday said with a smile.

"And I matched with two people, and I went on dates with them. One was to a delicious restaurant. And on my other date, we went to a farmers' market and to a bar with a hundred craft beers on tap."

"And are you going to go on any second dates?" Jack asked.

"Well, I don't want to see the first guy again," Willow admitted. "Ever, if possible. And I haven't made plans with the second guy yet."

Jack dramatically hit his forehead. "You see what your mistake was, don't you?" Willow paused. She actually did see what he was talking about. She hadn't made future plans for a date with Griffin officially, but she was sure they planned on going out again. She thought that they would talk about it over one of their morning coffee chats. It was true they hadn't had one that morning, but that was because he was going out to pick up some last-minute supplies for the house. He wanted to get some hinges that were slightly smaller for the office cabinets.

"You went to a place with a hundred types of beer, and you said you had a good time?" asked Jack.

"Yes."

"You should have suggested that you go back there. I'm assuming that you didn't try all one hundred of the different types. You could have said that you needed to try more of them. Perhaps it could have even become an activity for the two of you to try and taste all of them. It was the perfect *in* to continue seeing each other."

"She has an in because he's still finishing redoing her house," Wednesday added.

"That's an interesting in," Jack said, nodding. "Well, I think this is decent progress."

"She's trying really hard," Wednesday agreed.

Willow sighed. She didn't think they meant to make fun of her, but they were making her feel inept. She wasn't hopeless at dating. She had been married before even if that hadn't worked out. She was still young. She was successful with her business. She'd been called cute before. Okay, yes, this was usually because people were amused to see a petite person like her working with Irish wolfhounds. Still, she was attractive enough.

She just needed to remind herself that she wasn't really here to learn how to attract the opposite sex. She was here to learn about Jack and Kaitlin as a couple.

"Jack, do your first dates often lead to second ones?" she asked. "Or was Kaitlin a rare exception?"

"Kaitlin was an exception to everything," he muttered. "But we're here to focus on you. Let's celebrate your progress."

The celebration began by busting out a bottle of champagne, but the focus soon stopped being on her. Instead, it turned into a social media photo shoot.

Jack began by showing the "the proper" way to open a

bottle of champagne. Then he gave examples of the best way to make a toast. He explained how the speaker should be entertaining and yet modest. His speech about Willow finding true love ended up being about his business. However, Wednesday seemed to think it was fun. They took pictures of the champagne shooting out, clinking glasses together, and short clips of their toasts.

In the mini clips, Jack suggested they drink to his business. Wednesday toasted to living life to the fullest. Willow said that she was thankful for the champagne.

After their drinks, they dropped into some chairs. After making sure that he would get plenty of likes with the photos, it seemed like Jack was ready to talk to Willow again.

"Now," he said, "are you more interested in pursuing a single relationship? Or playing the field?"

Willow thought about it and decided to answer honestly. Maybe he would actually give some good advice. "I suppose I'd rather date one person I care about. But I want something casual at first."

Jack nodded. "That's tricky. You want compassion without commitment. You don't want either extreme. You don't want the consequences. Do you know how your beer-fan date feels about relationships?"

Willow set her jaw. Dating coach or not, she didn't like discussing this. She didn't know all the answers and, even if she did, she wasn't sure she felt like sharing anymore.

"I'll have to ask him on my next date," Willow grumbled.

"Maybe we could double date this week?" Wednesday suggested. "I'm sure I could find a date, and it could make for a fun post."

"Just remember the pointers I gave you at the picnic," Jack said. "Not that you really have to work to attract a man's attention."

"Wait a second," Willow said. "What picnic?"

"Didn't you see my posts?" Wednesday asked, sounding a little hurt.

"I guess I stopped looking once I knew why you blew Dad and me off for dinner."

"Okay," Wednesday said, sounding a little abashed. "I don't blame you for not seeing them. Jack crashed my picnic."

"Is there something going on between you two?" Willow asked, looking back and forth between them.

"No way," Wednesday said with a little laugh.

Jack also said no, but looked a tad affronted by Wednesday's response.

"I just mean," Wednesday said quickly, "that we met for a cross-marketing promotion. We wanted to reach more of an audience. If you get a chance, you should look at the post. It's kind of adorable. We had reverse picnics for our pictures. I had a red cup and a white plate. His cup was white, and his plate was red. That sort of thing."

"These pictures seem like they need a lot of planning," Willow said.

"Not always," Jack said. "I like to keep several picnic

baskets ready to go when the weather is warm. It seems like a spontaneous romantic trip."

"That you carefully calculated," Willow said.

Jack shrugged. "I am an expert."

"And it was fun," Wednesday said.

"I did learn some interesting things there though," Jack said. "I didn't know that you were so close to Terry."

Willow looked at her sister who mouthed the word "sorry."

It was Willow's turn to shrug. "I'm training her dog."

"You know all about her past with Kaitlin?" Jack asked. "Because your friend is the person I'd put my money on as Kaitlin's killer."

"I don't think she did it," Willow said. "And I know all about her past with Kaitlin. I'm not so clear on yours with her."

"We dated," he said. "What else is there to know?"

"Maybe why you had to keep it a secret?" Willow said, locking eyes with him. "Or about her carrying your child?"

Jack stood up and walked to the other side of the room. He seemed to be gathering his thoughts. Finally, he walked back towards them.

"Look," he said, "I'm not a monster. I wasn't going to abandon her with the baby."

"Even though you couldn't have been the bachelor king anymore?" Willow asked, rising to her feet.

"It might not have been good for my brand," he admitted.

"But part of what I teach people is when they move from dating to a relationship there are responsibilities. I was going to be responsible. I loved her, you know."

"Honestly, I don't know that," Willow said. Wednesday joined Willow at her side.

"Look, we cared for one another, but we weren't good for each other. That's why we were off and on so much. We had chemistry but no compatibility. And she was impossible to live with."

"Oh, really?" Wednesday asked, crossing her arms. "Because she was pregnant?"

"Because she was a hoarder," Jack said, throwing his arms up in the air. "You don't know what it's like to stay with someone like that. I have a great sense of style. But my things were getting covered with old newspapers and garbage. But that wasn't the worst of it."

"I'd love to hear it," Willow said. "Even though this is making it sound like you have a motive."

"We had a cat. A cute little thing with white paws. And it died because it ate rotting cheese that Kaitlin left out. Even after that, she didn't show any signs of improving her home," Jack said.

Wednesday covered her mouth with her hand. Willow knew she must be thinking of Rover.

"That does sound like someone difficult to live with," she admitted.

"I know it sounds terrible to say out loud, but in some

ways, losing the baby was the best thing that could have happened. It forced us to face the issues in our relationship and finally end it."

"That does sound pretty harsh," Willow said.

"Even though we weren't together romantically, it didn't mean that we didn't check in with one another every so often. We did care."

She observed him. He appeared earnest. It didn't seem like there was any bad blood between him and Kaitlin anymore.

"Thank you for telling us this," Willow said.

Jack nodded. He wasn't looking as cheerful anymore, but he poured out another glass of champagne and took a drink.

"We should probably get going," Willow said.

"That's right," Wednesday said. "I'll make sure these photos are tagged correctly, and then I need to plan my next event."

"And maybe go to your job?" Willow suggested,

Wednesday brushed away the suggestion. "Stop nagging. I know what I'm doing."

The sisters headed towards the door. Jack followed them. He accepted one of Wednesday's excellent hugs. Willow allowed herself to be hugged one more time. Jack nodded as if it had improved.

Then, he asked, "Your date you might see again is Griffin Maynard, right? The one your sister mentioned?"

"I am going to see him again," Willow said confidently.

"Could you do me a favor? Could you try and gauge his feelings about the luxury retreat I pitched to him last week?"

"You want Griffin to go away on a retreat?"

"No," Jack said, with a laugh. "I want him to build my luxury retreat. I could give seminars on how to be more successful in dating and then my guests can mingle with one another. I found the perfect location just outside of town. It could be peaceful amongst all those trees, and I know he'd make something amazing. He's the most sought-after contractor in town.."

"You asked Griffin about this a week ago?"

"That's right. Tell him to let me know when he's going to say yes."

Willow nodded and walked out the door with Wednesday beside her.

"What's wrong?" her sister asked. "Was it because I let it slip about you knowing Terry? I am sorry. I didn't mean to. I've been distracted lately."

"No. It's all right," Willow said. "That ended up convincing Jack to talk to us. He wanted us to know his version of the story."

"And do you think he did it?"

"I don't know," Willow said. "His motive seems weaker after talking to him."

Wednesday nodded. She was obviously distracted by her next project for her feature, but Willow did get her to mention that she planned to write the bio for their father.

After that, Willow was happy to let her focus on her own tasks. She had her own thoughts to deal with as they walked.

Jack said that he had asked Griffin to take on a luxury project a week ago. That was before Griffin pulled out of her renovation project for the dog spa, but it might have lined up with when he first advised her against doing it.

Why hadn't he mentioned this project before? Why was it a secret? Was it possible when he realized she wanted to start dating, he used that so he could move onto another job? Was it possible that Griffin tricked her too?

17

T he next morning, the coffee was hot, but Willow was feeling steamed enough without drinking it. She hadn't slept well. She kept thinking about how Terry was going to be wrongfully arrested for murder if Willow didn't find some new clues. Griffin was also on her mind. She alternated between being afraid that Griffin wanted to jump into a serious relationship, which would jeopardize the friendship they had, and fearing that his idea that they start dating was more about escaping a contract than any real feelings of affection.

Telescope looked tired too. He must have been kept awake by her tossing and turning. He barely barked at all when Griffin arrived, and after saying a brief hello, he headed to his dog bed for a nap.

Willow admitted that she was glad Telescope wasn't going

to be in the room. She had a feeling that the dog wouldn't like some of the things she might end up saying. If Tele was there, it might feel like fighting in front of the children.

She resented how cheerful Griffin looked when he joined her in the kitchen. He had a bounce in his step and a grin on his face.

"The flowers look nice," he said, after seeing them on her kitchen counter.

"Yes," she said, looking at them too. "Why did you get them for me again?"

Griffin looked puzzled. "I thought you'd like them. Did I get the wrong type?"

"So, you just got them for me for no reason at all?" she pressed.

"I thought it was a nice way to start a date," he said slowly. "Why do I feel like I'm walking into a trap? Does this have something to do with the case you're working on?"

"I'm not working on a case," Willow snapped. "I'm just helping a friend."

"And I admire that," Griffin said loudly. "What's going on today?"

Willow took a deep breath, trying to contain her emotions. She needed to be clear when she presented evidence of his possible deception. She didn't want him to know how much this might hurt her.

"I spoke to Jack Grim yesterday," she said.

"Is he the killer?"

"No. I mean, probably not," Willow said. "But I did learn something from him."

"About dating?" Griffin asked, looking unsure.

"About a luxury retreat he wants you to build."

"Oh, yeah, that," Griffin said with a chuckle. "He already mentioned how he'd want to have lots of hidden areas where couples could be alone in the building."

"Why didn't you tell me about it?"

"Are you upset?"

"This was about a week ago?" Willow asked, hoping that she didn't sound upset.

"I guess so," Griffin said with a slight shrug.

"So, it was right before you decided to pull out of my spa renovations?"

Griffin laid a fist on the counter. "I didn't pull out of the renovations. I tried to have a conversation with you about whether the spa was the best choice for you."

"And now I think you had a conflict of interest in that debate."

"I already told you that I was interested in Benny's project."

"And now Jack's too?" she accused, moving towards him.

"Maybe," he said, stepping back. "Is that a crime?"

"It is if you're trying to break a contract."

He began walking around the kitchen. "I don't know what's going on right now. How am I breaking a contract?"

"The contract for the dog gym would grandfather in the

spa, but you didn't want to do it. You wanted to do Benny's exciting hotel job. And now maybe Jack's too," Willow said. "That's why you wanted to date, isn't it?"

"Because of Jack's resort?" Griffin asked.

"Please stop pretending that you don't understand what I'm saying," Willow said, trying to stay calm. "The reason you wanted to start dating is because you knew that I'd let you out of your contract if we did."

Griffin opened his mouth and then closed it. He shook his head. "I can't stop pretending that I don't understand. Because I don't understand. Do you realize how crazy you sound right now?"

"Now you're calling me crazy?" Willow had to admit that she was feeling crazy at the moment, but she was being pushed towards it. "If you weren't trying to keep Jack's renovations a secret from me, then why didn't you mention them when Terry brought him up?"

"Because I didn't think I had anything helpful to add. I only spoke to him for a few minutes on the phone. That didn't make me qualified to judge whether he was a killer or not."

"Or you didn't want me to know that you were trying to take on other projects."

Griffin closed his eyes and took a deep breath. "I'm not trying to date you to get out of your renovations. I'm trying to date you because I like you. Even when you're like this."

"I don't want to be used again," Willow said.

"When have I done that?" he asked.

Willow frowned. Her ex-husband had been an excellent manipulator. It wasn't until they had been married for several years that she realized it. She had trusted him, and he had betrayed her. He had taken care of all the paperwork that assured that he got to keep her original business in the divorce proceedings.

He had used her to get what he wanted. She had promised herself that it would never happen again. Maybe there was a chance that she would scare a nice man off. But, maybe there was a chance she could protect herself from a man who planned on breaking her heart as soon as he broke her contract.

"Benjamin used to—"

"I'm not your ex-husband," Griffin said, cutting her off. "I'm me."

"But you didn't want my extra renovations," Willow said. "And dating me would guarantee that you didn't have to do them."

"But that's your rule. Not mine," Griffin said angrily. "You're the one with the rule about not mixing your personal life and business. I would have been fine with working for you and dating you."

"Still, it's just a coincidence that you wanted to start dating right after you had offers for these other renovation projects?" Willow challenged.

"I've wanted to date you for a long time," he said.

"Sure," Willow said, crossing her arms.

Griffin didn't say anything. Instead, he marched out of the house. Willow stood in her kitchen, watching him go. Sorrow welled inside her, but she tried to ignore it.

She walked to the front door, ready to slam it closed. However, Griffin wasn't climbing into his truck to leave. He had something in his hand that he must have taken from the cab. He let the car door close with a thud and stormed back towards the house.

"Why did you come back?"

"I want you to read something."

"Our contract?" she asked. "Did you find a loophole?"

"Read it," he said.

Willow took the letter and unfolded it. She was confused. "What is this?"

"This is the letter I wrote to you in high school. The one where I confessed that I had feelings for you and that I wanted to date."

"You wrote this in high school?" she asked.

"I stuffed it in your locker, but you never said anything. I guessed you didn't feel the same way. I found it by the lockers and brought it home. I found it again right around the time you moved back to Pineview, and, well, parts of it still echoed with me. I thought showing it to you on one of our dates would be cute. We could laugh about it," Griffin said. "But now I just want you to notice the date. Because it was well before I had this renovation offer."

Willow looked up from the letter. "I never saw this."

"It had been years since I thought of it too," he said as his tone softened. "Until I found it while cleaning."

"No," Willow said gently. "I didn't forget about this. I never saw it."

"Never?"

"No."

"It fell out of your locker? Or got stuck somewhere?"

"I guess so," Willow said, holding firm to the letter. "I would have remembered this."

Griffin moved closer. Part of Willow was moved by what he had written, describing how seeing her in the hallway and joking about the bad cafeteria food was the highlight of his day. However, part of her was still scared of being tricked. This letter was the past, and she needed to understand what was happening in the present.

"This doesn't change anything," she said. "You could have brought this here just to convince me that you like me."

"Exactly."

"So that I would let you out of the contract," Willow finished.

"I give up," Griffin said, shaking his head. "I don't know what else I can say. I can tell you that I care about you. I can show you that I've felt that way for a while. If you don't believe me, you don't believe me. But I don't really think that's the case."

"What?"

"I think you're scared. And I wouldn't have thought it

after seeing the brave stuff you did while trying to catch a killer or how fiercely you fought for your business. But you are. You're scared of living your life fully in case something goes wrong again."

"Thanks, Dr. Freud."

"I'm going to go. You can stay here. You can play detective and hide with the dogs if that's what makes you feel safe," Griffin said. "However, if you feel like wanting to live your life fully, and you want me to be a part of it, you're welcome to find me. But I'm not going to be party to these delusions and accusations anymore."

Willow didn't have a good response, so she blew a raspberry at him.

"Bye, Willow," he said.

He headed to his truck, leaving her holding the high school love note and trying to keep her head high.

18

Wednesday sat at her computer desk at the police station. True, there was a pile of paperwork that was growing on it. However, she could still handle it. She would snap one picture of her looking distraught at the stack with a caption such as "Office Work and No Play" or "PaperWorking It!" Then, she would start attacking it all.

Wednesday was pleased with the picture. That should satisfy her fans for a little while.

Smiling at the thought of having adoring fans, she tried to decide what to work on first. Then, she realized it was obvious. Her dad was worried about his bio that she had to do. She might as well write that first and put his mind at ease.

She moved the mouse on her desktop so the screensaver of

a cat in a policeman's hat disappeared. She brought up a blank document and wrote "Chief Franklin Wells" at the top of it.

However, before she could write anything else, her phone let out a ding. Recognizing that chime to mean she had gotten a new email, she reached for her cell.

The email was from *Clickable ConTENt*. Wednesday bit her lip. Was there a problem with her story? She thought that she was doing great. People seemed to love all her posts, from Pilates to baking pizza with her cat. She had been making sure that her week was full of exciting things to share.

Maybe it was good news? Could they want to do more with her? Did they ever do "A Month in My Life?"

Actually, that might be too daunting. She wasn't sure she could keep up this pace that much longer. After all, she currently had only written three words in her father's bio.

"Stop wondering and open it," she muttered.

She clicked on the message and began to read. It started out well enough, praising her feature. However, then it went on to tell her that they needed to bump the finale of her "Week in My Life." They wanted to focus on a different story that day, one that would get more traffic. She skimmed through the part about her replacement, something about a B&B, and got to the end. The editor wanted to know if Wednesday wanted to finish her "week" a day early or if she wanted to do one final post two days after the original final day.

"Neither," Wednesday grumbled. "It's not a real week if you do either of them."

The final line complimented her again and then told her to respond with her decision.

This was so unfair. Wednesday had worked hard on this feature. She had been sacrificing time she should have spent on her job or helping Willow clear Terry. She thought that getting this feature meant that the online world was taking her seriously. What did they think was so important that it warranted moving her finale to another day?

After taking a deep breath, she reread the section about the story that they wanted to do instead. She was glad she did. Now she realized that the B&B they were referring to was the one that Kaitlin Janes owned and where she had been poisoned.

Clickable ConTENt was planning to do a big piece on the murder. Kaitlin Janes had apparently written an article about the "Best Tips for Traveling with Pets" last month. However, now a reporter had found out that Kaitlin had been personally responsible for multiple dogs' deaths.

Wednesday frowned. She hated to admit it, but this did sound like a good story. This story had a great overarching mystery about the killer not being caught yet. Beyond that, this was a huge scandal. The owner of one of the most pet-friendly bed-and-breakfasts, and a self-proclaimed dog expert, had been responsible for doggie deaths. It was shocking and intriguing. It was something that Wednesday herself would click on.

It did seem like great content. However, how true was it?

If Kaitlin had been killing dogs, how could Wednesday not have heard about it before? She was the police secretary and usually knew all the happenings in town.

There was no way that she could have missed something like this. She started pawing through the paperwork on her desk. After some poking and prodding, Wednesday located the files if not the information she was looking for.

She couldn't find anything in writing that claimed that Kaitlin was responsible for a pet's death. The only complaints against the B&B were from Linda Grego. They were general complaints about being unsafe and unsanitary. The reports were never completely followed through with because the B&B had seemed so spick and span. Was it possible that the complaint was only directed at Kaitlin's living quarters?

Wednesday jumped online and started looking into Linda's online life. She was proud of what she found. Maybe she should be an investigator and not the secretary.

Linda had been posting pictures of two Yorkshire terriers on her Facebook pages, but then after some quotes about love and loss, the pictures transitioned to only having one little dog in them. Wednesday also found a GoFundMe page asking for donations for a pet's surgery. Because of the rush deadline Linda had for it, the campaign had only reached about half of what she was asking for.

Wednesday checked the dates. Linda's complaints against Kaitlin's B&B had begun right after the GoFundMe was set up. This couldn't be a coincidence. The dog's death and the police complaints had to be related.

She texted Willow right away. She was sure that she would be awake. Even though her sister wasn't much of a morning person, she had been getting up to have coffee with Griffin while they did the reno work. They were probably talking about their date now, which was something Wednesday did want to hear all about – but after she shared what she had found.

"Wait a second," Wednesday said, before realizing that she hoped her followers never found out how often she talked to herself. "That's only one dog."

She sent another text to her sister. After all the digging she had done, she had only found a possible connection between Kaitlin and one dog. Were there more? What other dogs could have died?

The questions were racing through her head, and she was feeling impatient, and kept checking her phone. Why wasn't Willow responding right away? Was she too distracted by Griffin? That would be bad timing for a good couple.

Wednesday started searching for cat videos that looked like Rover to distract herself. She wanted Willow to tell her what they should do next with this knowledge. What should they investigate next?

Wednesday froze and then hit herself in the head. How could she not have thought of this before?

She looked for the contact information at the bottom of the

email she had been sent and placed a call. Her point-of-contact at *Clickable ConTENt* answered with a silky voice.

"This is Sherri Lee."

"It's Wednesday."

"It can't be. My calendar says—"

"No. It's Wednesday Wells. I'm doing the feature for you."

"Of course," the voice said as if there had never been a mistake. "Did you decide what day you want to do your finale? I'm sure you have something special planned. Did I mention how much people have been loving this feature?"

"That's great," Wednesday said happily.

"Now, when do you want to end it?"

"That's actually what I wanted to talk to you about. I've had an idea."

"I don't want you to think that you were doing anything wrong. We loved your feature. Really. We just want to focus all our attention on this poisoning and dog killer story because we think it will get a ton of hits. We want it to be the only thing we're pushing that day."

"I think it will get a bunch of hits too," Wednesday agreed. "And I want to be the one to tackle the story."

"We have a reporter already."

"Yes. But I'm already in town. I live here, and I know all about the complaints that were made with the police about the B&B."

"I suppose we wouldn't have to send anyone out there if we let you cover it," Sherri Lee said thoughtfully. "But this is a really big story. We want it to be sensational. There are dead pets at a charming B&B. We can say how she even fooled us with her article about pet tips."

"I can handle this," Wednesday assured her. "I have an in with the police and with the local dog trainer. I could even incorporate this search into the 'Week in My Life' feature."

"Beautiful blonde investigates poor dead pets," the other woman said, testing out how it sounded.

"I know I can do this," Wednesday said. "I can find out all the facts in this case. This can even be my grand finale. Let me have a shot at the Murder Dog House."

"Murder Dog House," Sherri Lee repeated. "I like the sound of that. All right. You've got your shot. Find us some juicy information for this article. We want it to live up to our name."

"I'll make sure it's very clickable."

"You better," Sherri Lee said amicably. Then she hung up.

Wednesday smiled. She had saved her finale and now had an even more impressive story to write. However, she didn't have very much time to do it.

She put the Linda files on top of the stack on Kaitlin's death. Her father's barely started bio was still on her computer, but she would have to finish that later. She had sleuthing to do!

19

Willow was determined not to focus on her fight with Griffin, but she was still having trouble focusing on her trip to the city council with Wednesday.

She didn't like to think that she might have overacted and ruined a potentially great relationship. She also didn't think that she was completely wrong in asking about his motives. He could have been trying to sweep her off her feet to get out of renovating the spa. She'd heard of crazier things that people did to get out of work.

She didn't like arguing with people in general and hated when it was with people she cared about, and she had to admit that she cared about Griffin. She was sure that they had both said some things that they regretted that morning.

For example, what did he mean that she wasn't living her

life fully? She was living her life. She was running a business, and taking yoga classes, and helping a friend stop being the prime suspect in a murder. That sounded like living to her!

"Did you hear what I said?" Wednesday asked.

"Huh?" Willow said. So much for not focusing on Griffin. Apparently, she hadn't been paying attention to her sister at all.

"How are we going to get Linda to talk to us?"

"Good question," Willow admitted. They had just arrived outside of the city council's office building and were ready to go inside and find Linda. They were supposed to have decided on the best way to approach her on their ride over, but Willow had been distracted.

"I need to make sure that I get all the facts right," Wednesday said. "Both for the police investigation and for my article. However, I also need to make sure that I get some juicy details for the piece."

"If Linda's dog died because of something to do with Kaitlin, then she has a motive for the murder. That's a pretty juicy detail."

"Yeah. But I don't expect her to outright admit that she killed somebody. We'll have to be sneaky about this," Wednesday said. "But first, let's take a pic."

Willow recognized the irony of taking a picture to post on social media while claiming to be sneaky but agreed to the picture. Wednesday made a hopeful face and crossed her fingers. Willow crossed hers too though it was partially because she hoped that no one following Wednesday online would realize why they were there.

"Come on," Willow said, as soon as her sister lowered her phone. She dragged her inside and they found the office marked L. Grego.

Linda looked up as they entered. "Can I help you two?"

"Hopefully," Wednesday said before casting a glance at her sister.

"We're following up on that complaint you made with the police about the bed-and-breakfast," Willow said quickly.

Linda gestured towards the chairs by her desk but frowned.

"It's a bit late for that, isn't it?" she asked. "I mean, the problem basically resolved itself."

"Because of her death?" Willow said.

Linda nodded as they sat down. "The B&B will either close or go to a new owner, and they won't be able to carry on like Kaitlin did."

"What do you mean by that exactly?" Willow asked.

"I mean – not to gossip – but she was a slob, and it got so bad that it became dangerous. I'm surprised there weren't constant complaints about her."

"The guest portion of the house was immaculate," Wednesday said.

"Yes. But Kaitlin wasn't," Linda said. She seemed to regret saying that and continued. "I'm sorry. But I don't see how discussing this anymore will accomplish anything."

Willow decided to just ask her outright. "Did Kaitlin have anything to do with your dog's death?"

Surprise crossed Linda's face, but then she nodded. She placed her hands on the desk to support her. "Yes. I know she did."

"You didn't mention that in your complaint," Wednesday said.

"It's very difficult for me to talk about this," Linda said. "And I thought the police would realize it when they investigated the complaint. Then, Kaitlin wouldn't be able to accuse me of slander or anything like that."

"What happened?" Willow asked gently.

"Kaitlin ran such a lovely bed-and-breakfast. The guest area really is stunning, and it's so dog-friendly. I thought the rest of the house would be too," Linda said. It was clear that she was trying to hold back tears. "Kaitlin was also a dog sitter. I had to go out of town for a weekend, so I left my babies with her."

Linda picked up a picture frame, and it obviously became harder for her not to cry. She showed the photo to Willow and Wednesday. It was of two Yorkies in matching sailor costumes. One had a blue bow in her hair, and the other had a tiny hat on his head.

"My Pepe and Pattie," Linda said wistfully.

"I've only met Pattie," Willow said, thinking of the small dog that Linda was so protective of at the doggie gym.

"I thought Kaitlin would be a great dog sitter," Linda said.

"But I was wrong. Her apartment was such a mess, and it turned out to be deadly. There was all this junk on the floor, and it was dangerous. Pepe and Pattie must have eaten something while they were there. Pepe died! And Kaitlin didn't even notice until I came to pick him up. I could have hit her, but I was too busy worrying about Pattie who was also sick."

"You mentioned that she had recovered from surgery," Willow said.

"When I came back for her, she was so sick. I took her to the vet, and he said that she had an obstruction. She needed surgery for it. It took my poor baby so long to recover from it, and it was very expensive."

"You set up a GoFundMe page," Wednesday said.

"That's right. I couldn't lose Pattie as well as Pepe, so I needed to get the surgery. But it did cost a lot. I tried to raise money from donations, but it didn't cover the whole cost. That's why I've been pushing my candle sales more. I even tried to sell them to that hyper employee of yours."

"But," Wednesday said, "I don't understand why you wouldn't have put this in your complaints."

"Kaitlin tried to say that it must have been something that I did that hurt them. She tried to say that my babies must have eaten what did that to them while they were home with me," Linda said, shaking her head. "She tried to say that it was my fault."

"But you're saying it was her fault," Willow said.

"It was. My dog died because of her. And I thought

that's what the police would discover when they looked into my complaints about it being unsafe," Linda said. "But I guess she knew about those complaints because she got a dog of her own soon after. She wanted to be able to say that her dog was able to survive there, so I must be crazy. That I must have been the one who did something to hurt my dogs. But the only thing I did wrong was to trust the wrong person."

She began to cry. Wednesday stood up and moved closer to comfort her. She placed an arm around her. Willow stayed in her seat and made eye contact with the sobbing woman.

"So, you're not very broken up about what happened to Kaitlin."

"I just wanted her shut down, so she wouldn't hurt others too," Linda said. "I didn't wish her dead."

Wednesday continued to soothe the woman. Willow pressed on with her questions.

"Your business card was found on some coffee grounds in her apartment. Can you explain that?"

Linda looked down. "I was mad when I sent that to her. But it was just outdated coffee. There wasn't anything that could have killed her. I just wanted her to feel bad about what she did. If she wasn't going to feel bad emotionally, I wanted her to have stomach pain."

"She ended up feeling worse than that," Willow pointed out.

"I don't even know if she drank the coffee I sent her,"

Linda said. "I haven't stepped foot inside her house since the day I went there to collect my dog's body."

"I can't imagine how terrible that must have been," Wednesday said. "I was panicked when my cat needed stitches. To picture her having life-saving surgery after discovering her brother was dead? I couldn't stand it."

Willow didn't want to imagine anything happening to Rover or Tele either. However, nothing could condone murder.

"All I wanted was for the place to be closed down," Linda said. "And it would have been better for everyone if that happened. I mean, look at how she died. Nothing she was doing could have been safe. She was apparently ingesting poison without knowing it. She could have hurt other people. I know she hurt other animals."

"Other pets died in her care?" Willow asked.

"Definitely," Linda said. "There must have been several."

Wednesday nodded to her sister subtly but then gave a tiny shrug. Willow got the message. Wednesday had also heard that other pets had died but had no knowledge of specifics or real evidence to back up the claim.

"Who?" asked Willow.

Linda blushed. "All right. I guess I don't know all the animals who have been injured. And maybe some owners did believe that it was their fault and not Kaitlin's."

"You don't know anyone in particular?" Willow said, growing less certain that there was anyone else.

"There was at least one person I know who had an incident. Truman Fitzpatrick lost his championship dog, Nero, because he stayed with Kaitlin. He didn't tell me all the details, but I know that it happened."

Willow tried not to frown noticeably. Linda wasn't proving to be a reliable witness. Truman's dog, Nero, was alive and well and going to be her main competition at the dog show.

Were the flaws in her story because she was so focused on covering up her guilt? It was time to discover if Linda had an alibi for the mornings that Kaitlin's coffees had been poisoned.

"You said that you never went by the bed-and-breakfast again," Willow said. "You didn't even stop there one morning to see if your complaints were resulting in changes?"

"No. I didn't go there. And I didn't poison her coffee grounds," Linda said.

Willow tilted her head as she realized that the council member had mentioned that the grounds were what was tampered with.

Linda continued. "And this week has been especially busy for me."

Wednesday looked nervous, and Willow knew she was wondering whether there would be even more paperwork for her to fill out.

"I've been doing some secret shopping in town, and I've been volunteering in the mornings. I'm helping with breakfast duty at the high school. One of the lunch ladies is battling cancer and hasn't been able to come in. Especially because I'm on the city council, I feel like I should pitch in and help."

"You were there every morning?"

"For the past two weeks, actually," Linda said.

"Do you have the person in charge of breakfast duty's contact information?" Willow asked.

"Why? You don't believe me?"

"No," Willow said. "It's because we've been looking for some more volunteer opportunities in town. Wednesday thinks it will be good for a feature she's working on."

Linda went through her drawers and found the phone number. She wrote it down and handed the paper to Willow.

Willow thanked her and left the office with Wednesday. Linda was looking at the picture of her dogs as they walked out the door.

Once they were on the street, Wednesday plucked the piece of paper out of Willow's hands.

"I'll call them," she said. "I actually might see if I can volunteer at the high school cafeteria. It could be good for my feature. I can take pictures of the good deed, and I can reminisce about my own high school days."

"They'd probably make you wear a hairnet," Willow cautioned.

Wednesday frowned. "I'll call them later. But what do you think about all that? It seemed like there was some good information for my article."

"I don't know how much Linda really knew," Willow said, thinking aloud. "We now know the story about what happened to her dog and where the rumors about other dead pets started.

However, she can't have been right about Nero. He hasn't been training at the gym since Terry and Lady Valkyrie have been using it, but he's entered in the Field Club Championship. A dead dog can't compete."

"Why would she lie about that?"

"Maybe so we would believe her about her complaints against Kaitlin," Willow suggested. "She doesn't want to be the only one with a problem with the victim."

"That's not the case though, is it? Weren't there several people with a motive?"

Willow nodded. "But, they're also starting to be eliminated because they have alibis. We'll have to check and see if that's the same case for Linda. But there's something else that she got wrong too."

"What?"

"She assumed that the coffee grounds were poisoned like we did at first," Willow said. "However, now we know it was the coffee that she was drinking directly that had the poison in it. Someone had to add it right before she drank from it."

"If Linda was at the high school, she couldn't have done that. No matter how strong a motive someone killing your dog may be."

Wednesday took out her phone and dialed the number Linda had given them. Willow nodded appreciatively. It was time to see if they could rule out another suspect.

20

Wednesday sighed when she returned to the police station. It seemed as if the pile on her desk had grown. Oh well, she could work on it some now. It was after hours, so she could have some time to focus completely on the paperwork. Tomorrow she could take some pictures at the high school serving syrup on the pancakes which would be great for her feature. Then, she could get some work done at the station before writing her article on the dying dogs at the B&B. After submitting that, she could do something fun in the evening to post about. Or maybe she and Willow could catch up on what they had learned.

Talking to the man in charge of the high school cafeteria had yielded two things. Wednesday had found out Linda had indeed been working at school every morning, so she couldn't have added the poison. Wednesday had also secured a volunteer position in the morning.

After that, she had done more research on any dogs that might have died while in Kaitlin's care. The veterinarians and animal shelters she had spoken to didn't tell her anything that made her think that there were other dead pets. However, she did get an adorable bell to put on Rover's collar as a "get well" present.

She pulled her chair back and was about to sit when she heard someone enter the room. Wednesday jumped. She thought she would be alone this late at night.

"You've decided to come in?" her dad asked, turning on another light.

"You scared me," she said. "Though I do realize how funny that is to say. It should be safe at the police station."

Frank didn't laugh.

"I didn't know you were working this late," Wednesday said.

"I've been waiting to ask you how my bio was coming along."

Wednesday kicked the ground. "I'd say I've got a solid start on it."

Frank walked up to her computer and moved the mouse, waking it up again. It showed the document she had been working on when she left earlier that day. The bio currently still only said, "Chief Frank Wells."

She smiled awkwardly. "Well, that is a good start, isn't it?"

Her dad didn't look amused. "Wednesday, this is serious work, and there are serious deadlines."

"I know. And I'm going to finish everything. *Seriously.*"

He sighed. "I want to support you with your online thing, but it's not supposed to get in the way of your real job."

"My online *thing* is a job," she said, gritting her teeth. "Not only is it how I can express myself, but it has the potential to be profitable, especially since I just gained an extra assignment from *Clickable ConTENt.*"

"You took on another project?" Frank asked, not containing his annoyance. "Aren't you busy enough?"

"I can handle it," Wednesday said. "Have I ever let you down?"

"No. You haven't. But I've never seen you this distracted before. And I can't have you jeopardizing the station's ability to run smoothly."

"I'm distracted because this is an amazing opportunity," Wednesday said, getting heated. "You keep saying that you're supportive, but it doesn't feel like it."

"I just don't think that you're ready to leave your day job for Instagram."

Wednesday clenched her fists. He was right, but it still hurt to hear it said out loud. She was just starting out as an influencer, and she knew that she needed time to grow. She had thought that her father finally understood what she wanted to do, but it seemed she was wrong. He was just being patronizing. He still saw her pursuit of being a social media influencer as a hobby. Maybe he didn't care what she did outside of work, but he wasn't actively proud of what she was attempting.

"Fine," Wednesday said. She sat down and faced her computer with emotions welling up inside. "I'll just get to work then."

Frank sighed and placed a hand on her chair.

"I just want you to put a little effort into my bio. I'd prefer that you don't spread information that makes me look bad."

"So, this is all about you and your bio?" she accused.

"Wednesday, this is part of your job," he said evenly. "And a lot of people are going to see this."

"I know. But I could write your bio in my sleep."

He shook his head, still looking grumpy. "I know. I can see that you've been gathering your information."

"What?" Wednesday asked as he gestured to the pile of files on her desk. "That's my paperwork."

"With the Linda Grego complaints on top."

"I was looking through them."

"I'll leave you to work on the bio," he said. "Try to be not too harsh."

"Dad, what are you talking about?" Wednesday asked. "You're an amazing detective."

He stopped walking and then turned towards her. He seemed surprised. Wednesday wanted to laugh.

"You think that I don't know that you're great?"

"But, those files?" he said. "Haven't you been looking

through them and seeing all the mistakes I've made through the years? The biggest one recently being that I ignored Miss Grego's complaints. Maybe Kaitlin Janes would still be alive if I had been a more thorough investigator."

"Is that's what's been bothering you?" Wednesday asked.

"I know now that I should have followed up on the complaints," he said sadly.

"Dad, that's not your fault," Wednesday said, moving directly in front of him. "I was the one who took down Linda's initial complaint. And all of her many complaints. If anyone is to blame, it would be me. However, I still don't think it was my fault. That bed-and-breakfast had a spotless reputation. The kitchen was incredibly well-kept too. Anyone who has been there will tell you that. It didn't seem like there was anything to back up her statement. It didn't make any sense at the time."

"You really think so?"

"Linda is a neighborhood watchdog. Combined with how often she complains about other meaningless things, I didn't think there was anything to her complaints. We didn't know then that Kaitlin was a hoarder. She kept that hidden in her private apartment, and the complaints didn't mention that we should look into her as a dog sitter and not as a hostess."

"Thank you."

"For what?"

"I was starting to doubt my instincts," Frank admitted.

"But you've made me realize that the evidence wasn't there at the time."

"And Linda didn't want to provide it all. She told Willow and me more about it this time. She said her dog died because of Kaitlin's messy house."

"She told you that?" he asked, sounding serious again. "Were you two investigating?"

"No," Wednesday said quickly. "We just went to talk to her about volunteering at the high school until the lunch lady is well enough to return to work."

"It just so happened that you wanted to ask her about what happened to be her alibi at the time that the poison would have to be planted?"

"What can I say?" Wednesday said. "I like to help out."

"Just make sure that you don't put too much on your plate," he cautioned.

"I'm not. Not really. The things I'm doing are all really part of the feature on my life. And the only new thing I added is to write about the dogs who died at Kaitlin's. But I'll spin that as part of my feature too."

Frank put a firm hand on her shoulder and led her back to her chair. She sat down and stared up at him.

"Don't you want to hear about my day?"

"It seems like I can find out all about it online," he teased. "And I'd rather see you get some work done tonight."

"But, that's what I've been trying to say. Everything I'm doing right now is a form of work."

"Well, I'd like to see you add a little more to my bio. Maybe write a sentence this time."

"Dad, you don't have to worry about this. I can write this in no time flat."

"Then, you should be finished quickly," he said.

She gave him a look. Juggling everything required that she control when she did certain projects. She had just started to feel inspired about the case. She wanted to organize her thoughts about what she had found out and start writing the story about the "Murder Dog House." Though based on what she had discovered, she was going to have to change that title.

"I'd rather work on my other project first. I can feel the inspiration for it. I actually feel excited to start typing it out."

"How about you channel that typing enthusiasm for the bio," Frank said. "And if you finish that, then you can have tomorrow morning off."

"Really?"

Frank nodded. "And then you can go and do whatever it is that Instagram influencers do."

Wednesday smiled and nodded. Then, she set to add something of substance to her dad's bio. He deserved something great.

21

The next evening, Telescope made a reassuring sound from the passenger seat of Willow's car. She took one hand off the steering wheel to pat his head. They had planned on visiting Wednesday, but Willow sure wished she had more to report from her day.

She felt like she was going in circles with her thoughts on the case, and she hadn't discovered any more clues. She had felt a little better at the dog gym when she was training that afternoon. However, that was marred too. Terry had called and said that she decided to put Lady Valkyrie's training on hold. Until it no longer looked like she was going to be charged for the crime, Terry thought that they were deluding themselves. She said that they couldn't focus on a championship until the shadow of the murder had lifted.

Willow couldn't begrudge her those concerns, but she hated it all the same. Focusing on the Field Club Championship had been a happy distraction when everything else seemed to be going wrong. Also, without the money, Willow's hand was going to be forced when deciding on the doggie spa renovations. She wouldn't be able to make the decision on her own.

Then again, it already seemed like she had lost her contractor for the job. The decided lack of Griffin in her life was something she was missing greatly.

He had still arrived at her house promptly on time for work. However, he had declined a cup of coffee and had gone straight to starting on the renovations.

When he finished for the day, he announced that the current repairs were all finished. The house as they had planned it was done.

Willow had expected them to celebrate when this announcement was made. She had thought they might make a toast (and she could joke about how much she learned from the stupid lesson with Jack), or they might have had a celebratory meal. However, instead, they had merely walked around the finished house quietly. Willow nodded as he pointed out what had been fixed.

Then, he had said goodbye and walked out the door.

Willow had wanted to say something to fix the situation, but she couldn't. She couldn't completely trust that he didn't have ulterior motives for wanting to date her. She knew it was possible that she was imagining these things, and that she was coming up with reasons to push him away, but she couldn't stop herself. Maybe she really did want to distract herself by solving crimes and playing with dogs instead of investing in something that could be scary.

Telescope barked. She patted his head again, thinking that he was trying to make her feel better. Too late she realized that he was reminding her to turn down the street to get to Wednesday's house.

"You're one smart dog," she said. "I should probably have let you drive."

Telescope wagged his tail in response. Willow turned her car around and headed down the right street. She parked and headed to the door.

She was dreading knocking on the door and seeing Wednesday's cheerful face ready to take some pictures of their girls' night. However, after the door swung open, Willow saw that she was in no danger of that. Wednesday looked miserable.

Willow hugged her right away.

"What's wrong?"

"'My life,'" Wednesday grumbled.

She led her sister inside and to the living room. Wednesday plopped on the couch and pulled a blanket around her. Willow followed suit. Rover bounded into the room, happy to see Telescope. He grudgingly accepted her friendly sniffs of his backside but kindly didn't reciprocate so the stitches in her tail wouldn't be disturbed.

Willow stopped looking at the animals and looked at her sister.

"What's wrong with your life?" Willow asked. She wasn't feeling too great about her own either and found the blanket comforting.

"The feature. *Clickable ConTENt* hated it."

"I thought they loved what you were doing."

"They did at first," Wednesday explained. "They liked all the posts I was doing and the pictures I was posting. But they didn't like what I wrote about the B&B. I explained how Kaitlin was a hoarder but how we only had concrete evidence that one dog had died."

"Those are the facts," Willow said.

"That may be, but they wanted more," Wednesday said sadly. "I gave them an article, and because it wasn't as sordid as I am sure they were hoping, I told them how I could include it in the feature I was already doing. But they didn't like that. They were so disappointed by what I did. They said they wanted something more hard-hitting."

"I'm sorry."

"The worst part was that they thought that the reporter they were going to send would have done a better job. I feel like such a failure."

"That's ridiculous," Willow assured her. "You're great at sharing stories, whether it's in writing or with photos. And you care about the truth. You were only going to say things that could be backed up."

"I guess so," Wednesday said. "But I still feel lousy."

"Me too," Willow admitted.

"Why for you?"

"Take your pick," Willow said, leaning back against the couch. "I have no suspects, no boyfriend, and no championship dog."

"It's tough to be the Wells girls these days," her sister said dramatically.

"I feel like we should do something, but I'm not sure what. Part of me wants to do some yoga to find some Zen, and the other parts want to get drunk."

"Well," Wednesday said, perking up a bit. "Why don't we do both?"

Fifteen minutes later, the sisters were on their way to Namaste A While Studio. They had left Telescope with Rover so the "cousins" could play together, and they planned on joining one of the drop-in classes last minute, regardless of what it was. They lucked out because the one they arrived for was a mixed-level yoga class, suitable for everyone.

They enjoyed the poses and synching their breath to the movements to try and gain inner peace. Willow appreciated working up a sweat and taking her mind off all her problems.

As the class ended, they all put their hands together and bowed their heads.

Willow rolled up her mat quickly and looked at her sister.

"Time to hit the bar?" Wednesday suggested.

Willow laughed and agreed. They headed over to the juice bar, and both selected a smoothie, not caring about the colors this time. Instead, they were looking for flavors that would be good to mix with the rum that they snuck into the studio in a special water bottle.

They accepted their smoothies and when the juice maker's back was turned, poured their special add-in to the mix. They clicked cups together and took a sip.

"I'm glad we did this," Willow said.

"Me too," Wednesday agreed. "I didn't want to stay cooped up in the house, feeling sorry for myself."

"Right. It's much better to feel sorry for ourselves when we're out and about," Willow joked.

"Do you think I've blown my opportunity to be an influencer? I convinced them that I would write a great story."

"If I'm completely honest, I don't know if this site is going to keep working with you. But that doesn't mean you've blown your shot in the field. People really *like* your posts."

"Thanks, Wills. I needed to hear that." Wednesday took a big sip of her drink and then said, "And I know things will work out for you too. Terry is innocent, and the police will realize that. Probably with some help from you. And then you can get back to focusing on training."

Willow nodded. Training Lady Valkyrie would make her feel better, but things wouldn't be completely right until she figured out what to do about Griffin. She debated telling her sister about the letter that Griffin had written to her in high school. It had been so sweet. How would she have reacted if she had seen it at the time? Would it have been easier than seeing it now and wondering if it was some sort of ploy?

She poured a little extra liquid from her special water bottle into her drink and mixed it up.

"Are you doing what I think you're doing?"

Willow turned around to see Miranda joining them at the bar. She had her hands on her hips.

Wednesday gulped. "What do you think we're doing?"

"Spiking your drinks?" the studio owner asked.

"Maybe," the sisters responded in unison.

Miranda laughed. "I don't mind. As long as you don't get too silly."

"We won't get silly," Willow assured her. "We're having a pity party."

"I'm glad you decided to do it here where your mood will hopefully be lifted," Miranda said. "Is there anything I can do to cheer you up?"

"You can join us," Willow said.

Miranda happily sat with them but opted for a virgin smoothie. "I still have a class to teach tonight, and I'm going to have to stand on my head."

"Maybe we should stay for that class too," Willow said

with a smirk. "Maybe if we stand on our heads, we'll have a new perspective and can figure things out."

"What do you need to figure out?" Miranda asked.

"Love, life, business," Willow said, rattling a few things off. "And a murder case."

"Plus, how to spin an article about an evil B&B killing pets when the facts don't quite match," Wednesday added.

"Are you talking about the dog-friendly bed-and-breakfast that Kaitlin owned?" Miranda asked.

Willow nodded.

"What dogs died?"

"We know of a Yorkshire terrier," Willow said.

"And someone was trying to tell us that Truman Fitzpatrick's show dog died," Wednesday said. "But Willow knows that he's signed up to compete in an upcoming event."

"Really?" Miranda asked.

"Um. Which part?" Wednesday asked.

"It's only that I thought Nero had passed away too," Miranda said. "Truman had come in here asking me for some sage. He didn't say it outright, but I got the sense that he had lost his dog. When I didn't see Nero for a few months, I thought it confirmed it. I'm very glad to hear that I was mistaken."

"It seemed like his dog had died?" Willow asked.

"He was acting like it. He was upset. But maybe the sage was for another dog."

Willow bit her lip. She tried to think. How often had she seen Truman and Nero in town recently?

"I should go and prepare for my next class," Miranda said, setting her smoothie down. "Thanks for letting me join."

"Thank you," Willow said, and she was very grateful. Miranda might have just given her the information she needed to figure out who the murderer was.

22

Back at the doggie gym the next morning, Telescope looked up at Willow as if he was questioning whether this was a good idea or not.

"It's going to be fine," she assured him. "I just need to see for myself."

She ruffled the dog's ears. She actually was feeling jumpy about her plan but didn't want to admit it. Instead of doubting her idea, she used her nervous energy to check that everything was in order in the back room of her doggie gym. This was the last place that Griffin had worked on in the dog area.

She willed herself not to think about Griffin as soon as that thought entered her head. She needed to keep sharp and stay focused.

The back room was mostly used for storage, and there was

an assortment of replacement parts for obstacle courses in case dogs of different sizes wanted to try a specialized run. There were extra chew toys and treats in the open, and there was a table where the dog trainers could sit on their breaks.

There was also a locked closet. Willow kept some "valuables" in there, meaning the more expensive pieces that she would hate to have stolen if a burglar made his way inside. This was also where she was keeping anything that could possibly have ill effects on the dogs. After all the talk of poison recently, she was being extra careful. She didn't keep any rat poison in the gym, but she did keep the cleaning supplies and extra cans of paint in the closet. After checking that everything was in order, she left her key in the lock. She didn't want her pockets to jingle when she had serious work to do.

After checking the back, she made her way to the main floor of the indoor dog gym and surveyed the area. Everything looked in place there. The obstacle course was just the way she wanted it to be.

"Hello, there," Truman said, waving as he entered the dog gym with his Irish setter.

"Hi," Willow said, keeping a smile on her face.

They walked up to her. Telescope was sticking close to her legs. He could sense the tension in the air.

"Is this true?" Truman asked. "Did you really set up a course according to the parameters of the Field Club Championship and you're going to allow me some private use of it?"

"That's right," Willow said, hoping she sounded convincing. "Terry hasn't been able to come in for a training session for a while, and I've been feeling that my setup is wasted. I was hoping I'd win you back as a customer if you liked using the space."

"It might just work," Truman said with a smile.

Willow looked at the Irish setter at his side. He certainly looked like Nero. He was the same size, his fur was a brilliant red, and his eyes were alert. However, it had been ages since she had seen the dog in person. She needed to be certain.

"Don't worry," Willow continued, as she realized she had been staring at the dog. "I won't stay the whole time and spy. That's not an admirable thing for the trainer of the competition to do."

"I appreciate that," Truman began.

"I just want to see a little bit of what Nero can do. It's been so long since I saw him."

"Well, he's the same old Nero."

The Irish setter looked up and tilted his head. He seemed to know that they were talking about him. He wagged his tail.

"Can he still do the high jump over the hurdle?" Willow asked, pointing to the tallest obstacle. "The one that won him some competitions."

"Of course, he can," Truman said.

"I'd love to see it."

Truman tried to suppress a smile. "Were you having trouble getting Lady Valkyrie to leap over it?"

"Maybe," she replied, looking sheepish.

"We can show off a little bit," Truman replied. He was looking pleased with himself as he led his dog towards the obstacles.

Willow ran a hand through her hair. This was going to be the moment of truth. She needed to see what Nero would do.

Truman called for the dog to begin the course. The Irish setter sailed over a few smaller easier obstacles. He seemed to concentrate more on the large ones but did make it over the high jump. He leaped straight over the hurdle and landed with only a slight thump.

Well, she had her answer. She walked over to the grinning Truman.

"Not bad, huh?" he said.

"That was pretty good," Willow said. "Of course, he's not quite as good as your last dog."

"What?" Truman asked, surprised.

"Your last dog. Nero."

"This is Nero," Truman said defiantly.

"No," Willow said, shaking her head. "He's not."

"Can you even hear yourself? What do you mean he's not Nero?"

"He might be *a* Nero, but he's not the Nero that won those competitions in the past," Willow said coolly. "And I think it might have been bad form to name your new dog the same name."

"What makes you think he's a different dog?" Truman crossed his arms, keeping the leash in one hand.

"That high jump," Willow explained, pointing at it. "The first Nero used to wag his tail while going over the top. It was a subtle movement, but I always noticed it. This dog doesn't do that."

Truman's eyes narrowed. "Is this why you invited me over here? To try and trick me?"

The Irish setter ran up to them, seeking attention. Willow kneeled down and patted him on the head, calmly saying, "I wanted to see what he could do."

"I trained the tail wag out of him," Truman said. "You must not be a good enough trainer to know how to fix something like that."

Willow ignored the comment and focused on the dog. He had allowed his tongue to roll out of his mouth happily as she petted his head. This allowed her to get a good look at his teeth.

"Did you also train away his age?"

"What?" Truman asked.

"Nero was almost three years old," Willow explained. "But based on this dog's teeth, he's not even two. I know the Field Club focuses on athleticism instead of a judge's examinations, but if I could recognize this, other dog experts could as well. He's too young to be Nero."

"But, they said…" Truman trailed off, and pointed a finger

angrily towards her face. "You're trying to get my dog disqualified from the competition. I won't let that happen."

Willow stood up. "I was trying to determine whether Kaitlin had killed your dog or not."

Truman froze. Finally, regaining some composure, he asked, "Where did you hear that?"

"From Linda. She also lost a dog because of Kaitlin's negligent care while she was puppy sitting," Willow said. "Miranda also had a suspicion that was what happened. You should be more careful who you buy sage from."

"That's not conclusive," he said.

"It will be easy to test this dog and see if he's the same one that won the championship or not," Willow said. "It's clear to me he's a different dog. And Linda already told me that Nero died under Kaitlin's care. Why lie about it?"

"Look," he said, "I have a contract to breed Nero. You don't understand what Kaitlin took from me when she let him die under her care."

"And what was that?"

"Nero wasn't only my dog and friend. He was the source of my income. I lived off his championship win money and from his breeding contracts. Do you know how much money I would be out?"

"So, that's why you didn't report Kaitlin?" Willow asked. "You thought it was more cost-effective to replace your dead prize-winner with a phony?"

Willow continued to pet the dog. It wasn't his fault what his master had done. He was a good boy.

"I'm not proud of what I did," Truman said. "But I did what I needed to do."

"Is that why you killed Kaitlin too?"

"What?" Truman asked, taking a step back. "I didn't kill anyone."

"You did," Willow countered. "And you hoped Terry would take the blame."

"If Terry takes the blame, it's because she looks so guilty. She is guilty! Look at her history. Look at what she did when she was involved with the pageants. She has a history of playing dirty. I didn't know what underhanded thing she'd try, but it looks like she's trying to get you to shift the blame to me. It's not going to work. Terry is the killer."

"No. She's not."

"It's a shame too," Truman said. "All her tricks didn't work out. She'll be in jail during the competition. Lady Valkyrie will never win now."

"I hate to tell you this," Willow said, "your new Nero is a very sweet boy, but he's no winner. He doesn't have the spark that his predecessor had or the smooth landing."

"He'll do fine."

"He won't win against Lady Valkyrie. And, of course, she's still competing. Regardless of what happens to Terry, she's still going to run. Do you think I would be willing to give up on the championship?" Willow thought she could be excused for telling a white lie in the interest of catching a killer.

Truman turned pale. "You're still competing?"

"You have no chance of winning," Willow said, hoping to taunt him into a confession. "He's not a winner, and neither are you. And you're not a very good schemer either. I figured out what you did, and I'm sure the police will too."

Willow was hoping that she would make him angry enough to admit to the crime. Instead, she had put him into a rage that warranted attacking her. He lunged at her and she ducked under his arm and stepped out of his reach, narrowly escaping. Nero and Telescope started barking.

Truman wasn't finished. He continued after Willow as she raced away. A plan formed in her head quickly. She knew she was in better shape than Truman. If she could get him into the proper spot, then she thought she knew a way to contain him.

She ran towards the back room of the doggie gym and opened the closet door before Truman and the dogs could catch up with her.

She was about to yell a taunt to lure the dog breeder into position when he stumbled into the room. Feeling confident about her plan to get him into the closet, she allowed him to come closer. She was about to dodge away when he did something unexpected and terrible.

He swung the leash he was still holding around her neck and pulled. She felt the leather tightening around her neck and tried to gasp for breath.

Fear began to set in. Everything was backfiring. She had wanted to catch the killer. She hadn't wanted to give him an opportunity to kill again!

Her knees buckled, and she felt the world starting to fade away. She wasn't making sense of what Truman was saying in her ear, but she knew it wasn't kind words.

Then, she saw a white ball of fur running towards them. It was Telescope zooming forward to come to her defense.

He sunk his teeth into Truman's ankle and the man yelped. He loosened his grip on the leash, and that was all Willow needed to resume her fight.

Coughing, Willow jerked the leash further away from her neck. She elbowed Truman as hard as she could. He stumbled backward, and she escaped his grasp. She gave him a final push, and he fell into the closet. Heaving for breath, Willow locked the door. She leaned against it and slowly slid down until she was sitting on the floor.

Telescope ran up to her, and she hugged him close.

"Good boy."

"The next time you want to catch a killer by yourself—"

"Wait for backup?" Willow suggested.

"Don't follow through with the impulse," Frank said.

Willow was seated in his office, making a statement about what had happened. Her father had told her that Truman had confessed, so she probably wouldn't have to appear in court. But she was eager to hear more about the confession and fill in the gaps in what she knew. However, it seemed she would have to listen to a lecture first.

"I'm sorry I worried you, Dad. But I was perfectly fine. I had the situation under control."

Frank moved closer and looked at the marks on her neck.

"I did," she said, covering the bruises with her hand. "I had Tele as back up."

"I should give that dog a medal. After all the times he's saved your neck," Frank muttered. "Literally this time."

"I could put it on his collar," she said with a smile.

Frank just shook his head.

"I promise I won't do this sort of thing again," Willow said. "If…"

"If?"

"If you tell me the details of Truman's confession."

This time Frank had a slight smile. "You don't have it all figured out?"

"I knew Truman was the killer," Willow said. "As soon as I realized that his champion dog had died under Kaitlin's care, I realized that he was the one to poison her. He wanted to frame Terry too. That's why he started using the rat poison the day she came into town. But when did he actually add it to the coffee?"

"Do you really promise not to get into these situations again?" he asked, leaning on his desk.

"To the best of my ability," she said, thinking that was fair.

Frank realized that was as good as he was going to get. "Will you at least promise to always have that dog of yours with you?"

"That I can definitely promise."

Her father sat at his desk. "Truman Fitzpatrick used to date Kaitlin. That's how he learned about her past relationship with Terry Gib and how to get into her apartment undetected. He was furious with her when his dog died under her care."

"I would be too," Willow admitted.

"He thought that he would be able to kill Kaitlin and frame Terry for the crime, getting rid of his competition and enemy at the same time. After Terry Gib arrived in town, he snuck into Kaitlin's B&B and laced the coffee every morning. He knew her routine and put the poison in her mug when she walked her dog in the morning. He was going to add the poison again the morning she died, as usual, but it was no longer necessary."

"But you found rat poison in her mug that day," Willow pointed out.

"She must have re-used a mug."

"That's how it happened," Willow said with a nod. "I was hoping he'd tell me. But he opted for another plan of attack."

"Will, I hope that you already know this."

"That her being a hoarder worked as part of his plan? He wanted the traces of rat poison to be found to implicate Terry."

"That I care about you," Frank said.

Willow smiled and blushed. "I know that, Dad."

"You and your sister are the most important things in the world to me," he continued. "I don't know what I'd do if I lost you. Please don't make me face that."

"I won't," she said, quietly. "I'm sorry I scared you."

He got up again and patted her shoulder. "I know you didn't mean to. And I don't mean to sound harsh when we have the proper killer in custody because of your efforts. But try to imagine how you would feel if you lost somebody that you cared about."

Willow nodded. She realized it wasn't that difficult to imagine. She was already afraid that she had lost someone.

"Dad, do you mind if I sign my statement tomorrow?" she asked. "I have someone I need to talk to."

Frank raised an eyebrow.

"Someone who I think being with feels right."

23

Two months later, Willow began her morning like she did every day – with a cup of coffee. However, there was something different about this particular morning.

"What are you smiling about?" Griffin asked as he refilled her cup.

"Well, I do have a lot to smile about," Willow said coyly. That was certainly true. In the few weeks since Terry had been cleared of the crime, there had been a lot of activity, but almost all of it had been positive.

"Really?" Griffin asked, playing along. "Do you?"

"There was that Field Club Championship," Willow said, taking a sip of her coffee.

"Right. I seem to remember something about that," Griffin said, pretending to be deep in thought.

"Yes. It was yesterday."

"And how did that go for you?" he asked, playing dumb.

"My dog came in first place. Lady Valkyrie blew everyone else out of the water."

"I bet it had a lot to do with her trainer."

Willow smiled at the compliment. She was proud that they had done so well. Despite all the chaos that occurred during their training, they had still pulled it off. She planned on hanging her copy of the blue ribbon in her office, right next to her framed picture of Tele on the day she adopted him.

"Of course, I do have other things to smile about too," Willow said.

"Really?"

"Sure," she said playfully. "There's all the good news that my family has received. Wednesday won over *Clickable ConTENt* again by having a kickass story about how Kaitlin's killer was apprehended. They liked it even though she only used true facts."

Griffin laughed.

"And my dad's bio was successful. It actually impressed some higher-ups and reminded them of everything he's done for the force and the town," Willow continued. "I might also be smiling about how other things in town seemed to work out as well."

"And what things would those be?"

"Well, Kaitlin's dog, Polly, found a forever home with Linda Grego. She has two dogs that she can dress up in matching outfits again. And Nero II is going to stay with Terry."

"I think that's pretty nice that she's taking in the dog of the man who tried to frame her for murder."

"It wasn't the dog's fault," Willow said. "And she knows how to handle Irish setters."

"Is his name going to stay Nero II?" Griffin asked.

"Well, Terry has been calling him Nearly as a nickname instead. She thought the whole ordeal was a close call that we nearly didn't escape from."

"That was especially true for you," Griffin said.

Willow shrugged it off and then returned to her little game. "Of course, there is one other thing I could be smiling about."

She moved closer to Griffin, and he put his arms around her.

"And what could that be?" he asked.

"Last night," she said simply.

Griffin was smiling too. "I have to admit that I enjoy our morning coffee chats together even more when it follows a night together."

"Me too," she agreed.

He kissed her. She still felt the same fireworks that she had felt after their first kiss. Their relationship was moving at a pace that she was comfortable with. They hadn't proclaimed their feelings toward each other to the world, but they were clearly dating.

Griffin was still looking happy when they pulled apart. However, then he put a serious look on his face and took a step away.

"I'm afraid there is still something that we need to discuss. Now that you've won the championship."

"What?" she asked, feeling nervous. Things had seemed to be going so well. She tried not to let her familiar panic about relationships take over. She reminded herself that she trusted Griffin and that their time together still felt right.

"We've danced around the edges of this for a while. However, now you actually have the money for it," Griffin said. "But I'm afraid I'm going to have to officially turn down the job of the doggie spa."

"Oh," Willow said, relaxing. "That's all right. I've decided to pass on the project too."

"Really?"

She nodded. "I think I have enough on my plate without adding grooming to it as well. And it's true. My heart isn't really in it."

"If you want my opinion," he said. "I think you're making the right decision."

"I know I am," she agreed. "This does open up another opportunity for me. I do have all those dog show winnings I could use, and I was thinking of using them on another renovation project."

"What's that?"

"My master bedroom," she responded with a wink.

They both started laughing. They fell into an easy conversation and continued to enjoy their coffee. Willow couldn't help thinking if all her days started this way, she might just become a morning person after all.

END OF "BARK UP AND SMELL THE COFFEE"

PAWS FUR PLAY BOOK TWO

Home is Where the Bark Is
July 5 2018

Bark Up and Smell the Coffee
September 6 2018

The Bark of the Town
November 1 2018

PS: Keep reading for an exclusive extract from **The Bark of The Town.**

ABOUT STELLA

Stella lives and breathes cozy mysteries! With her head always buried inside these books, it's no wonder that she would put pen to paper to bring her own cozy mysteries to life. The words flew onto the page, and she's already teeming with ideas for the next cozy mystery series.

With her trusted canine by her side, it seemed only natural to be inspired by her beautiful beagle Doogle and the many hours they spent walking through scenic New England villages. When Stella's not reading books, she's off on road trips, exploring every nook and cranny in neighboring towns, seeking inspiration for her next book.

She's keen to see what her fellow cozy critics think of her new cozy mystery so please leave a review and share your thoughts with Stella.

Get three cozy mysteries for FREE when you sign up to Stella's Mailing List!

MEET DOOGLE!

I would like to thank you for purchasing this book. If you would like to hear more about what I am up to, or continue to hear about Olivia's superb sleuthing—then please sign up for my mailing list at www.StellaStClaire.com.

Most importantly, you will get the cutest Beagle around hitting your inbox every month. Doogle the Beagle is my awesome canine companion and not a line of cozy mystery goodness would get written without him. He's quite a talker, so I'll let him introduce himself...

I'm no Sherlock Bones, but when it comes to Cozies, I know my stuff. Every plot pawblem Stella has, she comes to me. She talks, I listen and before you can say *Labracadabrador* she's off typing again. Stella and I are a pretty good team—even if I have to do all the hard work...

BLURB

Willow Wells is just beginning to feel settled back in her
hometown. She has a thriving business, a hot boyfriend, and
the support of her family. Things couldn't get better. Until it all
comes crashing down when two of the town's mean girls are

found murdered. Not only are Willow and her sister Wednesday first on the scene for both murders, Wednesday is the prime suspect.

Suddenly, Willow's perfect life is falling apart. To give Willow time to solve the crime, her boyfriend Griffin has taken over her dog gym business. Willow's father, the rock of both the town and the family, is suddenly powerless to help. And, worst of all, the evidence against Wednesday is mounting.

Willow will have to face her past and the reason she left Pineview all those years ago. If she doesn't solve this case— and solve it fast—then the future she's worked so hard for will end up dead and buried.

The Bark of the Town
Pre-order your copy at
www.stellastclaire.com

EXCERPT

"Look," Willow said, attempting to give a rousing speech. "I know this seems pretty disheartening right now, but it's all going to work out. I already discovered a possible motive for the murders. I'm sure whoever is on the case now will find even more. And will find the evidence to convict the real killer. And then everything will go back to normal."

Frank made a noise of discontent. "I'm not so sure of that."

"What do you mean?" Willow asked.

"It means that I'm not confident in the detective that they chose to lead this case," Frank said, angrily poking his side dish with his fork. "It's Clint McMillen."

"Who's that?" Griffin asked, looking at everyone around the table.

"A detective that Dad never really got along with," Willow answered.

"I don't think I've ever really explained to you the source of this bad blood between us," Frank said, crossing his arms.

Willow shook her head and tried not to be obvious about gritting her teeth as she prepared to hear bad news.

"The job means everything to McMillen and in general, he's been pretty good at it. He hoped that it would become a family tradition and that his children might follow in his foot-steps. And I can understand that."

Willow looked away. She had always felt bad about disap-pointing her father and not becoming a detective. When she was younger, she showed a great aptitude for it, and she was still good at solving puzzles today. And while she had helped solve two cases since she moved back to Pineview, she had learned a long time ago that it wasn't the right job for her. The mistake that led her to this conclusion still haunted her. Her father might be disappointed that she changed careers, but she was glad that he didn't know the real reason for her decision.

"And McMillen's daughter, Megan, did join the force. He was very proud that she was working her way up the ranks. However, it came to a stop when I caught her cheating on her detective's exam. It didn't thrill me to have to be the one to turn her in, but I felt it was my duty to report it. I feel like every officer on the job needs to earn their rank honestly."

"Of course," Wednesday seconded.

"She was barred from becoming a detective," Frank continued. "And McMillan blames me for ruining his daughter's career and his dream of a family of officers. It's obvious he's had a vendetta against me for quite some time."

"But, he's blaming the wrong person," Griffin said, putting a fist on the table. "He should be mad at his daughter for cheating. Not at you for trying to uphold the integrity of the force."

"Logically, that's true," Frank agreed. "But fathers don't like to blame their children."

"But he's a cop. He'll still do his job, won't he?" Griffin asked. "If he does some investigating, he's sure to find evidence that points to someone besides Wednesday."

"He will still do his job, but we have to admit that there is a lot of circumstantial evidence that implicates Wednesday," Frank said grimly. "She was found with both of the dead women and had blood on her hands."

"I was checking for signs of life," Wednesday said, sounding dismayed.

"I know," replied their dad. "I know you didn't kill anyone. But I think Detective McMillen wouldn't be unhappy if they made a case against you."

Willow listened to the exchange, but she had been lost in her own thoughts as well. Hearing the story of how Megan McMillen had embarrassed her father made her breathe a silent sigh of relief that she had quit trying to become a detective when she did. Her mistake as an intern on the Pineview Police Force had been terrible – a suspect had been tipped off by her actions.

She kept thinking how grateful she was that her error had never come to light. She was glad that she hadn't embarrassed her father on the force.

She was just thinking what a good thing it was that she didn't go further into detective work when her father said, "Willow, I'd like to ask you to investigate these crimes."

"What?" Willow asked, thinking she had misheard him.

"I'm afraid that McMillen might try to hang this on Wednesday out of revenge. I need someone to look at this case objectively. Or," he conceded, "objectively enough. I'd be all right with you assuming that your sister is innocent."

"Because it is the truth," Wednesday added.

"Since I've been put on leave, I can't do anything via the station," Frank said. "If I can't investigate, I need someone who can."

"You are kinda great at this," Griffin said, grinning at her. "You saved me before."

"I trust you," Wednesday said. "I bet you could figure out who really did this."

Willow didn't answer right away. She had intended on poking around and finding some clues to help the police and point them in the right direction. However, now this request felt official. She wasn't sure how she felt about that. She didn't want to make a major mistake like she had when she was an intern with the police. It still haunted her that the culprit had been able to elude capture because of her error. What if something like that happened again? Could she live with that guilt?

But, on the other hand, she couldn't not try and help her sister, regardless of the circumstance or her doubts. She couldn't let Wednesday be railroaded for something she didn't do.

Not knowing about her secret mistake from her past, Griffin must have thought that the cause for delay was because of how busy she'd said she was earlier.

"Don't worry about the dog gym," he said gallantly. "I can watch it and make sure everything runs smoothly. That way you can devote as much time as you want to the investigation."

"Well, of course, I'll help Wednesday," Willow said, realizing she needed to say this out loud.

She wasn't going to leave her sister hanging – especially if she was the only suspect the station had.

The Bark of the Town
Pre-order your copy at
www.stellastclaire.com

MORE BOOKS BY THIS AUTHOR

VISIT WWW.STELLASTCLAIRE.COM

Made in the USA
Monee, IL
26 July 2021